AN EVENING
WITH CLAIRE

GAITO GAZDANOV

AN EVENING
WITH CLAIRE

Translated from the Russian and with a Foreword
by Bryan Karetnyk

PUSHKIN PRESS

LONDON

Pushkin Press
71–75 Shelton Street
London WC2H 9JQ

An Evening with Claire was first published as *Вечер у Клэр /
Vecher u Kler* by J. Povolotzky & Co. in Paris, 1930

This translation first published by Pushkin Press in 2021

1 3 5 7 9 8 6 4 2

ISBN 13: 978-1-78227-605-0

Frontispiece: Gaito Gazdanov in the 1920s

Designed and typeset by Tetragon, London

Printed and bound in Great Britain by TJ Books Limited,
Padstow, Cornwall on Munken Premium White 80gsm

www.pushkinpress.com

CONTENTS

FOREWORD

December 1929. The blackening, unassailable reality of Soviet rule in Russia and, for the myriad Russian refugees scattered throughout Europe and the Far East, the vanished hope of returning to the dreamscape of their past. In exile, a raging cultural battle against the new proletarian art threatening to devastate centuries of tradition, and growing fears over the viability of a national literature raised abroad.

For a decade already the exiled grandees of pre-revolutionary letters have been espousing a mission to preserve the undisfigured legacy of Russian culture—but survival is predicated on evolution, and the path ahead seems as perilous as it does obscure. Now the old guard is beginning to atrophy, ceding to new and younger writers, to the children of revolution, for whom Russia is but a fading memory. Irina Odoevtseva's *Isolde* has just been published; Vladimir Nabokov's *The Luzhin Defense* is being serialized; and three debut novels—Nina Berberova's *The Last and the First*, Yuri Felsen's *Deceit* and Gaito Gazdanov's *An Evening with Claire*—are on the cusp of publication. Each of these remarkable works will stand in its own way as a feat of literary innovation in exile, yet none more than Gazdanov's will so captivate the émigré spirit and light the way.

When Gazdanov completed his manuscript in the summer of 1929, he was a mere twenty-five, but had resided in Paris by then for over six years and had not seen his homeland in almost a decade. The docks at Saint-Denis, the railway tracks, the factories in Javel—the arduous years of manual labour and destitution were now at an end: by day he studied at the Sorbonne; by night he drove a taxicab. What few hours remained he devoted to literature, and by the time that *Claire* finally materialized that December, he had published a handful of short stories in the European émigré press. None of this, however, could have prepared him for the literary sensation that *Claire* would provoke. Its tender, tragic evocation of a past lost among the ruins of revolution and civil war struck a nerve across the diaspora, winning success among the reading public and critics alike. A relative unknown before the work's publication, Gazdanov gained instant celebrity in the weeks and months after, vaunted as the new lodestar of émigré literature.

Readers of the work should not find it difficult to see why this was so. Gazdanov's novella literally and symbolically straddles past and present, Russia and

Europe, classicism and modernism. Critics saw in it the marks of both Ivan Bunin and Marcel Proust, and even dubbed Gazdanov a *prustianets*—a "Proustian" *à la russe*. The epithet is apt, for the novella's stream-of-consciousness narrative, circular episodic structure and thematic preoccupations with the creative workings of memory are inseparable from Gazdanov's nostalgic, semi-autobiographical account of a childhood spent travelling across the length and breadth of the former empire—from St Petersburg to the Caucasus, from Minsk to Siberia, ending on the war-torn Tauric Peninsula, by the shores of the Black Sea, as the Civil War reached its fatal close. Yet for all that, *An Evening with Claire* defies neat categorization. It is, by turns, a memoir, a romance, a human document, a fairy tale, a history of the soul, a casebook of mental illness, a *Bildungsroman*, an odyssey. It exists simultaneously on rival planes, between the real and the irreal, between historical fact and literary fiction, between memory and dream, mixing them so as to render any distinction meaningless. The novella is, in short, the very epitome of what it meant to be a young émigré, caught between two worlds, at home in neither, forever lamenting what has been lost while never losing sight that something vital may yet be gained.

B.S.K.

AN EVENING
WITH CLAIRE

All my life has been the gauge of our inevitable tryst.

ALEXANDER PUSHKIN

CLAIRE WAS ILL. For whole evenings I would sit up with her, and, each time I left, I would invariably miss the last Métro and end up going on foot from the rue Raynouard to the place Saint-Michel, in the vicinity of which I lived. I would pass by the stables of the École Militaire; from there I could hear the clanging of the chains to which the horses were tethered and smell that thick equine aroma so uncommon in Paris; then I would walk along the long and narrow rue de Babylone, and at the end of this street, in a photographer's shop window, by the dim light of a distant street lamp, the face of some famous writer, composed entirely of slanting planes, would gaze out at me; those omniscient eyes behind horn-rimmed European spectacles would follow me for half a block—until I crossed the glittering black strip of boulevard Raspail. At length, I would arrive at my *pension*. Industrious old women dressed in rags would outstrip me, tottering on feeble legs. Over the Seine myriad lights would burn brightly, drowning in the darkness, and as I watched them from a bridge, it would suddenly seem to me as if I were standing above a harbour and the sea were covered in foreign ships emblazed with lanterns. Taking one last look at the Seine, I would go up to my room, lie down to sleep and sink instantaneously into the unfathomable gloom where trembling bodies stirred, not always quite managing to take on the form of images familiar to my eyes and thus vanishing without ever having materialized. And even in sleep's embrace I lamented these disappearances, sympathized with their imaginary, unintelligible sorrow, and so I lived and slumbered in an ineffable state, which I shall never understand in waking. This fact ought to have grieved me, but in the morning I would forget what I had seen in my dreams, and my abiding memory of the foregoing day would be the recollection that I had again missed the Métro. In the evening I would set out again for Claire's. Several months previously her husband had left for Ceylon, leaving us alone together; and only the maid, who brought in tea and biscuits on a wooden tray decorated with a finely drawn image of a gaunt Chinaman, a woman of around forty-five who wore a pince-nez (and hence didn't at all look like a servant) and who was forever lost in thought—she would always forget the sugar tongs, or the sugar bowl, or else a saucer or a spoon—only she would interrupt our ménage, coming in to ask whether *Madame* needed anything. Claire, who for some reason was sure that the maid would be offended if she didn't ask her for something, would say: yes, please bring the gramophone and some records from *Monsieur's* study—although the gramophone was quite superfluous and, once the maid had gone, would remain in the very spot where she had left it, while Claire would immediately forget all about it. The maid would come and go around five times during the course of an evening; and when I once remarked to Claire that while her maid looked remarkably well preserved for her years, and though her legs still possessed a positively youthful indefatigability, all the same, I wasn't too sure that she was quite all there— either she had a mania for locomotion or else her mental faculties had almost imperceptibly but unquestionably been attenuated in connection with the onset of old age; Claire looked at me pityingly and replied that I should do better to exert my singular Russian wit on others. Besides, as she saw it, I ought to have remembered that only the previous day I had shown up again in a shirt with mismatched cufflinks, and that I couldn't, as I had done the day before that, simply throw my gloves down on her bed and take her by the shoulders, something that wouldn't pass for a proper greeting anywhere on earth, and that if she wanted to enumerate all my violations of the elementary rules of propriety, then she would have to go on for... at this point she paused in thought and said: five years. She uttered these words with a look of severity; I began to feel sorry that such trifles could irk her so and wanted to ask her forgiveness, but she turned away; her back began to convulse, and she raised a handkerchief to her eyes—and when at last she turned to look at me, I saw that she was laughing. She told me that the maid was seeing out the latest in a series of romantic liaisons, and that a man who had promised to marry her now refused bluntly. That was why she was so lost in thought. "What's there to think about?" I asked. "So he's refused to marry her. Does one really need so much time to grasp such a simple thing?"

"You always put things much too plainly," said Claire. "Women do. She's thinking because it's a pity for her. How is it that you can't understand this?"

"Was it a particularly long affair?"

"No," replied Claire, "two weeks in all."

"Strange, she's always seemed so lost in thought," I observed. "Just last month she was every bit as unhappy and in reveries."

"Good grief," said Claire, "that was another affair of hers."

"It's really quite simple," I said. "Forgive me, but I wasn't aware that your maid's pince-nez masked the tragedy of some female Don Juan who actually wants to tie the knot, as opposed to the Don Juan of literary renown who took a rather dim view of marriage…" But Claire interrupted me, reciting with great pathos a line that she had spotted on a billboard, the reading of which had reduced her to tears of laughter:

Heureux acquéreurs de la vraie Salamandre
Jamais abandonnés par le constructeur.[1]

The conversation then returned to Don Juan before passing somehow on to ascetics and Archpriest Avvakum; however, upon reaching the temptation of Saint Anthony I paused, recollecting that Claire didn't much care for such talk; she preferred other subjects—the theatre, music—but most of all she loved humorous anecdotes, of which she knew a great many. She would recount these exceedingly witty and thoroughly obscene yarns, after which the conversation would take a rather queer turn, and even the most innocent of phrases would seem to conceal double-entendres—and Claire's eyes would begin to sparkle; but when she stopped laughing, her eyes would grow dark and criminal, and her delicate brows would knit together. I would move in closer, and she would whisper angrily: *mais vous êtes fou*[2]—and so I would retreat. She would smile, and her smile would blithely say: *mon Dieu, qu'il est simple!*[3] Then, picking up our interrupted conversation, I would start to inveigh against things towards which I normally felt absolute indifference; I would try to sound as cruel and insulting as possible, as though craving revenge for the defeat I had just endured. Claire would agree mockingly with all my arguments, and my defeat would be all the more obvious because she conceded so readily. "*Oui, mon petit, c'est très intéressant, ce que vous dites là,*"[4] she would say without taking the trouble to conceal her hilarity, which, incidentally, pertained not at all to my words, but to that very defeat, and by emphasizing that disparaging "*là*" she made clear that she didn't attach the slightest significance to anything I had to say. Making a supreme effort, recognizing that it was now too late, I would again resist the temptation to draw nearer to Claire and would force myself to think of other things. Her voice came to me half-muffled; she was laughing and telling me all manner of nonsense that I heard out with rapt attention, until I realized that Claire was simply having some sport. It amused her that in such moments I was incapable of understanding anything. I would come to make amends the following day; I would promise myself not to sidle up to her and to choose such topics that would eliminate any danger of repeating the previous evening's humiliating moments. I would speak of all the sorrows I had known, and Claire would grow quiet and serious and, in her turn, recount the death of her mother. "*Asseyez-vous ici,*"[5] she said, indicating the bed—and I sat down right beside her while she rested her head in my lap, saying: "*Oui, mon petit, c'est triste, nous sommes bien malheureux quand même.*"[6] I listened to her, fearing to move lest my slightest movement offend her grief. She stroked the quilt first one way, then the other; and it was as if her sorrow were being spent in these caresses, which were unconscious to begin with but then drew her attention and ended in her noticing the hangnail on her little finger and reaching out for the nail scissors lying on the bedside table. Once again she smiled a lingering smile, as if she had caught and traced within herself some long train of memories that ended on an unexpected, though by no means unhappy, thought; and Claire regarded me with momentarily darkening eyes. Gingerly I transferred her head over to the pillow and said: I'm sorry, Claire, I've left my cigarettes in the pocket of my trench coat—and went out into the hallway as her quiet laughter followed me from the other room. When I returned, she remarked:

"*J'étais étonnée tout à l'heure. Je croyais que vous portiez vos cigarettes toujours sur vous, dans la poche de votre pantalon, comme vous le faisiez jusqu'à présent. Vous avez changé d'habitude?*"[7]

And she looked me in the eyes, laughing and pitying me, and I knew then that she understood perfectly well why I had stood up and left the room. What was more, I had the carelessness then to extract my cigarette case from my back trouser pocket. "*Dites-moi*," said Claire, as though imploring me to tell her the truth, "*quelle est la différence entre un trench-coat et un pantalon?*"[8]

"Claire, that's very cruel," I replied.

"*Je ne vous reconnais pas, mon petit. Mettez toujours en marche le phono, ça va vous distraire.*"[9]

That evening, as I left Claire's, I heard the maid's voice coming from the kitchen—trembling and faint. She was wistfully singing a jolly little ditty, and it took me by surprise:

> *C'est une chemise rose*
> *Avec une petite femme dedans,*
> *Fraîche comme la fleur éclose,*
> *Simple comme la fleur des champs.*[10]

She instilled so much melancholy into these words, so much languid sorrow, that they began to sound different, unusual, and the line "*fraîche comme la fleur éclose*" instantly recalled to me the maid's aged face, her pince-nez, her love affair and her eternal pensiveness. I mentioned all this to Claire; she took an active interest in the maid's misery—for nothing of the sort could ever happen to her, and this sympathy demanded none of her own emotions or anxiety—and she was terribly fond of the little ditty:

> *C'est une chemise rose*
> *Avec une petite femme dedans.*

She would imbue these words with the most diverse inflections—now questioning, now confident, now triumphant or mocking. Whenever I heard this motif on the street or in a café I would begin to feel out of sorts. Once I went to see Claire and started to curse the song, saying that it was much too French, that it was trite and that no self-respecting composer would be taken in by the allure of its cheap showiness; this encapsulated the main difference between the French mindset and serious things, I said: this art, so unlike real art, is as a fake pearl is to the genuine article. "It lacks the most important thing," I said, having exhausted all my arguments and losing my temper. Claire nodded in the affirmative, before taking my hand and saying:

"*Il n'y manque qu'une chose.*"[11]

"And what exactly is that?"

She laughed and sang:

C'est une chemise rose
Avec une petite femme dedans.

When Claire was convalescing and, having spent a few days out of bed, sitting in an easy chair or on the chaise longue, began to feel quite well again, she asked if I would accompany her to the cinema. After the cinema we sat for an hour or so in an all-night café. Claire was awfully short-tempered with me, and interrupted me often: if I made a joke, she would hold back her laughter and say, smiling despite herself: "*Non, ce n'est pas bien dit, ça*"[12]—and, since she was in what appeared to be a foul mood, she projected her own dissatisfaction and irritability onto the world around her. She would ask me in astonishment: "*Mais qu'est-ce que vous avez ce soir? Vous n'êtes pas comme toujours*"[13]—although I was behaving no differently than usual. I saw her home; it was raining. When I kissed her hand at the door, taking my leave, on a sudden she said irritably: "*Mais entrez donc, vous allez boire une tasse de thé*"[14]—and she said this in such an angry tone, as though meaning to drive me away: well, what are you waiting for, can't you see that I'm sick and tired of you? I went in. We took our tea in silence. I felt awkward, and so I went over to her, saying:

"Claire, there's no need to be angry with me. I've waited to be with you for ten years. I'm not asking anything of you." I felt like adding that such a long wait entitled me to the least modicum of kindness; but Claire's eyes had turned from grey to almost black; with horror I saw—for I had waited too long and ceased hoping for this moment—that Claire was right beside me and that her breast was pressing against my buttoned-up double-breasted jacket; she took me in her arms, her face drawing nearer; the chilling fragrance of the ice cream she had eaten in the café suddenly struck me incongruously; and she said: "*Comment ne compreniez vous pas?...*"[15]—and a shiver ran through her body. Her misty eyes, endowed with the capacity for so many metamorphoses—cruel one moment, but shameless or laughing the next—these murky eyes of hers I saw before me for a long time. When she had fallen asleep, I turned over to face the wall and was visited by a former sorrow; this sorrow hung in the atmosphere, and its transparent waves rolled over Claire's white body, over her legs and breasts; it escaped her mouth in an invisible breath. I lay there beside her, unable to sleep; drawing my gaze from her blanched face, I noticed that the midnight blue of the wallpaper in Claire's room seemed suddenly brighter and strangely altered. The dark-blue that I saw in my mind's eye had always reminded me of a mystery that had been solved—the solution to which had been obscure and sudden and seemed to halt before having revealed itself completely: it was as if the force of some spirit had stopped in its tracks unexpectedly and died, and in its place there had arisen a dark-blue backdrop. Now it had metamorphosed into something brighter; as if the force were not yet finished and the dark-blue colour, having brightened, had found within itself an unexpected, matt-despondent hue, which curiously chimed with my feelings and undoubtedly had some connection with Claire. Pale-blue spectres with lopped-off hands sat in the room's two easy chairs; they were coolly hostile towards one another, like people whom the same fate has befallen, sharing the same punishment but for different misdemeanours. The wallpaper's lilac border meandered in an undulating line, like the hypothetical path of a fish swimming in uncharted waters; and through the fluttering curtain by the open window a distant current of air was forever trying to reach me but could not; it was of that same pale-blue hue, and carried with it a long gallery of memories, which fell as regularly as raindrops, and just as irrepressibly. But Claire turned over, awake now, and mumbled: *"Vous ne dormez pas? Dormez toujours, mon petit, vous serez fatigué le matin"*[16]—and again her eyes dimmed. She lacked, however, the strength to overcome her torpid slumber and, scarcely having uttered this phrase, fell back asleep; her brows remained raised, and as she dreamt she looked surprised by what was happening to her. There was something exceedingly characteristic in this surprise: in surrendering to the power of sleep, or of sorrow, or of some other emotion, however strong it might be, she never ceased to be herself; and even the mightiest of shocks seemed incapable of altering anything in this so exquisite a body, of destroying this final, invincible charm that had compelled me to spend ten years of my life searching for Claire, never forgetting her, no matter where I found myself. "But in any love there is sorrow," I recalled. "Sorrow for the end and the approaching death of love, if it has been a happy one, and, if the love has been in vain, sorrow for the inviability and loss of what was never ours." And just as now I lamented the riches that I didn't have, so had I once grieved for Claire when she belonged to another; and so now, as I lay on her bed in her apartment in Paris, amid the pale-blue clouds of her room, which until this evening I would have deemed impossible, imaginary, the clouds which surrounded Claire's alabaster body, covered as it was in three places with such shameful and agonizingly alluring hair—so too, now, I grieved for the fact that I could no longer dream of Claire as I had always dreamt of her, and that much time would pass before I could construct for myself another image of her, one that would become, in its own way, just as unattainable for me as until now had been this body, this hair, these pale-blue clouds.

I thought of Claire, of the evenings I had spent with her, and gradually I began to remember everything that had gone before them; and the impossibility of under-standing and expressing all this weighed heavily on me. That evening it seemed more apparent than ever that no amount of effort would allow me suddenly to embrace and conceive of that endless succession of thoughts, impressions and sensations, the whole assemblage of which rose up in my mind like a row of shadows reflected in the murky and fluid mirror of indolent imagination. It was to music that I owed the most wonderful, most sear-ing emotions that I ever experienced; but I can only ever aspire to its enchanting and momentary essence—I cannot embody it. So often at a concert I would suddenly begin to understand things that had eluded me until then; the music would unexpectedly awaken in me such strange physical sensations that I had believed myself incapable of feeling, but with the final dying notes of the orchestra those sensations would vanish, and once again I would find myself in the state of ignorance and uncertainty that was so essential to me. This malady, which would create for me an improbable dwelling between the real and the imaginary, resulted from my inability to distinguish the efforts of my imagination from the genuine, spontaneous emotions that events aroused in me. It was a kind of absence of spiritual touch. In my eyes every object was almost deprived of its definite physical contours; and by dint of this peculiar deficiency, I was never able to produce even the feeblest attempt at drawing; later at school, try as I might, I never could envisage the complex lines of a diagram, although I understood perfectly the purpose of their combination. Yet my visual memory had always been well developed, and to this day I do not know how to reconcile such a glaring contradiction. This was the first of innumerable contradictions that would later plunge me into impotent reverie and reinforce an awareness that I was incapable of penetrating to the very core abstract ideas; and this awareness, in turn, would engender self-doubt. I was for this reason very timid, and my childhood reputation for being insolent could be explained, as indeed several people (my mother, for instance) saw it, by precisely this ardent desire to vanquish a nagging feeling of self-doubt. Later on, I developed a habit of associating with the broadest possible range of people and even elaborated certain rules of intercourse which I almost never transgressed; these consisted in the deployment of several dozen topics of conversation that, to all appearances, were sufficiently complex, but in actual fact were exceedingly primitive and accessible to anyone; nevertheless, I always found the essence of these simple concepts, so conventional and inevitable, strange and uninteresting. I never did manage to overcome my own cheap curiosity, however, and took enormous pleasure in provoking certain people to candour. Their humiliating and worthless confessions never aroused what might otherwise have been my rightful and understandable disgust. They should have done, but never did. Perhaps this was because it was rare for me to experience strong negative feelings about anything, so indifferent was I to extraneous events: my oblivious inner existence held an infinitely greater significance for me. When I was a child, at least, this existence was more firmly anchored in the outer world than it was later; but gradually it distanced itself—and in order to return to this dark expanse with its thick, palpable air, I would have to traverse a distance that grew in proportion to the life experience I accrued: that is, put simply, my store of observations and visual or olfactory sensations. Every now and then I would think with horror that, perhaps, at some point in the future, the day would come when I should no longer be able to return to myself and would turn into an animal—and with this thought, a canine head would never fail to appear in my memory, devouring scraps from a rubbish heap. However, that perilous convergence of the real and the imaginary, which is what I considered my malady to be, was never far away. Sometimes, during feverish bouts of delirium, I would find myself unable to apprehend my own true existence; a din and clangour would assault my ears, and in the street I would have such difficulty walking, such difficulty as if I, with all my great weight, were struggling to push on through the dense air, through the bleak landscapes of my fantasy, where the startled shadow of my head glided so effortlessly. At such moments memory forsook me. It had always been the least perfect of my faculties—the fact that I could easily memorize whole pages of printed text notwithstanding. It would drape a transparent, glassy web over my recollections and destroy their magnificent quiescence. My emotional memory was immeasurably richer and more potent than my rational one, but never was I able to delve as far back as my original feelings and learn what they were.

I became conscious of the world and first began to understand its principles when I was six years old; when I was seven, thanks to the relatively large quantity of books that were kept under lock and key, but which I still managed to read in spite of this, I developed the facility to set my thoughts down in writing; it was then that I composed a somewhat long story about a hunter of tigers. I have preserved the memory of only one event from my childhood. I was three years old at the time; my parents had briefly returned to Petersburg, which they had left not long before; they expected to remain there for only a short while—something in the way of a fortnight. They stayed there with my grandmother, in her large house on Kabinetskaya Street—the very same in which I was born. The windows of the apartment situated on the third floor gave onto a courtyard. I recall being left alone in the drawing room and feeding my toy bunny a carrot that I had procured from the cook. Suddenly, odd sounds issuing from the courtyard caught my attention. It sounded like a quiet growling, broken occasionally by a metallic ringing that was very subtle but distinct. I went over to the window, but no matter how I strained on tiptoe to catch a glimpse of whatever was making the noise, nothing came of it. I proceeded to wheel a large armchair over to the window, clamber on top of it and from there climb up onto the window ledge. Even now I can see the desolate courtyard below and the two woodcutters moving back and forth in turn, like poorly fashioned mechanical toys. Sometimes they would stop, pausing for breath, whereupon the sound of the suddenly halted and now vibrating saw would reverberate. I watched them as if transfixed and unconsciously crawled out of the window. The whole upper half of my body dangled over the courtyard. The woodcutters saw me; they stopped without uttering a word, lifting their heads and looking up. It was the end of September, and I remember suddenly feeling a gust of cold air; my arms, no longer covered by the sleeves that I had pushed back, began to freeze. At that point my mother came into the room. She quietly walked over to the window, picked me up, shut the window—and fainted. The episode is lodged in my memory with exceeding clarity. And I recall now yet another instance, which took place significantly later—both of these memories instantly transport me back to childhood, to that period in time which I am no longer able to comprehend.

This second incident consisted in the following: after I had learnt to read and write, I read in a little children's book a story about a village orphan, whom, out of kindness, a teacher took into her school. He helped the caretaker to heat the stove, cleaned the rooms and studied diligently. Then one day the school burnt down and, come winter, the boy was left out on the street in the bitter frost. No other book since has left such an impression on me: I saw this boy before my very eyes, saw his late mother and father and the burnt-out ruins of the schoolhouse; and my grief was so intense that I cried for two full days, ate almost nothing and barely slept. My father finally lost his temper and said:

"See, see what comes of teaching a boy to read so early. He ought to be running about, not reading. Glory be, there'll be time enough for that. Why on earth do they print stories like that in children's books?"

Father died when I was eight years old. I remember how Mother once brought me to see him in hospital. I hadn't seen him for a month and a half, not since the very onset of his illness, and I was struck by his emaciated face, his black beard and burning eyes. He patted me on the head and, turning to Mother, whispered:

"Take care of the children."

Mother couldn't bring herself to answer him. Then he added with unusual force:

"Good God, if only they could tell me that I could be a simple shepherd, just a shepherd, but that I'd live!"

After that, Mother sent me out of the room. I went out into the garden: the sand crunched beneath my feet; it was hot and bright, and I could see far into the distance. Sitting in the calèche with Mother, I said:

"Mama, Papa looked quite well. I thought he'd look much worse."

She didn't reply, but only pressed my head to her lap, and like that we rode home.

There was always something inexpressibly delightful about my memories: it was as if I no longer saw or knew what was happening to me beyond the particular moment I was reanimating. I would find myself by turns a cadet, a schoolboy, a soldier—and that was all: everything else would cease to exist. I grew accustomed to living in a past reality that my imagination resurrected. My powers within this past reality were infinite; I submitted to nobody, to the will of none; for hours on end, lying in the garden, I would create fictitious situations for all the people in my life and force them to do as I pleased, and this perpetual amusement of my fantasy gradually formed a habit. Directly, however, came a time in my life when I lost myself; I lost even the ability to recognize myself in the self-portraits that I drew. During this period I read voraciously: I remember the frontispiece in the first volume of Dostoevsky's collected works. They confiscated this book from me and hid it away, but I broke the glass door to the bookcase and from its great multitude of tomes I extracted the very one with the author's portrait. I read everything indiscriminately, although I cared little for the books that I was given to read, and I loathed the "Golden Library" series, except for the fairy tales by Andersen and Hauff. At that time my individual existence was almost imperceptible to me. Reading *Don Quixote*, I would imagine everything that happened to him, but the work of my imagination would go on in spite of myself; indeed, it required almost no effort whatsoever. I took no part in the heroic deeds of the Knight of Sorrowful Countenance, nor would I laugh at him or at Sancho Panza; it was as if I were not there at all and Cervantes's book were being read by somebody else. I believe I could compare this period of concerted reading and development, this epoch of my totally unconscious existence, to the most profound psychic syncope. Only one feeling remained with me, a feeling that ripened in those days and subsequently never left me, one of transparent and distant sorrow, unwarranted and pure. Once, having run away from home and finding myself walking through a reddish-brown field, I spotted in a far-off ravine, glittering in the spring sunlight, a layer of snow that had yet to melt. A delicate white light suddenly rose up before me and seemed so impossibly beautiful that I could have wept with emotion. I made my way towards the spot and reached it several minutes later. Dirty soft snow lay upon the black earth, but it shimmered faintly with a bluish-green light, like a soap bubble. It was nothing like the glittering snow that I had seen from afar. For a long time afterwards, I recalled that snowdrift and the feeling of *naïveté* and sorrow I experienced then. And several years later, as I read a very moving book that was missing its title page, I envisaged that vernal field and the distant snow, and the few steps it had taken for me to see its dirty, melting remnants. "And is there nothing else?" I asked myself. For that was how life then seemed to me: I would live out my allotted years on this earth only to arrive at my final moments and die. But how could this be? Was there nothing else? These were the only stirrings of my soul to happen during this time. Meanwhile, I read foreign writers, saturating myself with the stuff of strange lands and times, and gradually this world became my own: and I came to see no difference between Spanish and Russian settings.

I awoke from this condition a year later, not long before I was enrolled in the gymnasium. By then all my feelings were familiar to me, and what followed was merely an outward expansion of my knowledge—so insignificant and so inessential. My inner life was beginning to emerge in spite of my immediate circumstances, and all the changes that occurred in it did so in darkness, utterly independent of my marks for behaviour and my punishments or failures at school. Those times of complete self-absorption passed and paled and returned to me but rarely, like bouts of a remitting but incurable disease.

My father's family often moved from place to place, not infrequently crossing vast distances. I remember the toing and froing, the packing of unwieldy items, and the eternal questions of what exactly had been packed in the trunk containing the silver, and what in the one containing the furs. Father was always cheerful and carefree, while Mother forever wore a look of severity; it was she who took charge of all the packing and travelling. She would glance at her little gold watch, which hung, according to the fashion of the day, on her chest, and was always afraid of being late; and Father would calm her, saying with an expression of surprise:

"Come now, we still have masses of time."

He himself was always late for everything. Whenever faced with the necessity of going away, he would recall the fact three days beforehand and say: well, this time I'm going to be punctual—and without fail, having kissed us goodbye, my younger sister with tears in her eyes, he would return home half an hour later.

"I simply don't understand how it could have happened. By my reckoning, I had fourteen whole minutes to spare. There I arrive at the station, only to be told that the train has just pulled out. It's astonishing."

He was forever busying himself with chemical experiments, geographical surveys and social questions. They consumed him so entirely that he often forgot the outside world—as if nothing else existed. Still, there were two things that never failed to rouse his interest: fires and hunting. Fires revealed in him an extraordinary energy. He would retrieve whatever he could from a burning building, and, since he was awfully strong, on several occasions he in fact managed to rescue from the flames whole cabinets, which he would carry out on his back. Once, in Siberia, when a house belonging to a certain wealthy merchant was ablaze, he even managed to carry a fireproof safe down a wooden ladder. As it happened, not long before the fire broke out, he had asked this very merchant to lease him one of the apartments in another of his houses, but the latter, upon learning that Father was not a man of business, had refused out of hand. After the fire, the merchant came to see us and asked Father to move into that house—he even brought some gifts with him. Father had forgotten all about the fire by then; he was glad to be of service to anyone, but it was not mere sympathy for those in need that spurred him to action: indeed, he harboured an unfathomable love of fire. Meanwhile, the merchant insisted. "How could I have known that you would rescue my safe?" he kept repeating naïvely. At last Father realized what the merchant was talking about; he lost his temper and sent him packing, with the words: all this is stuff and nonsense, and I'm a busy man.

He relished physical exercise, was a fine gymnast
and an indefatigable rider. He always laughed at the
"seat" of his two brothers, both officers in the Dragoon
Guards, who, as he was wont to say, "never did learn to
ride a horse properly, even by the time they passed out of
that most equestrian of academies; then again, even as
children they never were adept at riding, and only went
to that horsey academy of theirs because you didn't have
to study algebra there." He was a first-rate swimmer, too.
At a deep point in the river, he would do a most remarkable thing, the likes of which I never saw again: he would
sit, as though on land, and raise his legs so that his body
formed an acute angle, and suddenly he would begin to
spin like a top. I remember how I would sit naked on the
shore and laugh, and later on, clutching Father's neck,
I would cross the river atop his broad, hairy back. Hunting
was his passion. Sometimes he would return home on a
low, wide sleigh, having painstakingly tracked an animal
over the course of a whole day and night—and from the
sleigh the glassy, dead eyes of an elk would look up. He
hunted bison in the Caucasus, and he would think nothing of travelling several hundred versts just to take up an
invitation to go hunting. He was never ill, didn't know the
meaning of fatigue, and would sit in his study—filled, as
it was, with cases, flasks and retorts bearing some viscous

mass—for hours on end, only then to embark on a three-day hunt for wolves. Having slept little, he would return and resume his seat at his writing desk as if nothing had happened. He was possessed of prodigious patience. He spent a whole year's worth of evenings sculpting from plaster of Paris a relief map of the Caucasus, filled with the minutest of geographical details. One day, after the work was finished, I went into Father's study; he wasn't there. The map was sitting on the top shelf of the *étagère*. I reached up, pulled it towards me, and it came crashing down on the floor, shattering into pieces. Father came to investigate the noise, shot me a look of reproach and said:

"Kolya, you mustn't come into the study without my permission."

He then sat me on his shoulders and we went to see Mother. He told her that I had broken the map and added: to think, I'll have to do the map over from scratch. He set to work, and by the end of the second year the map was finished.

I knew my father but little, although I knew what mattered most about him. He loved music and could spend hours listening to it, never stirring or straying from his chair. The tolling of bells, however, he couldn't abide. Anything that even in the least reminded him of death remained forever strange and hostile to him; this also accounted for his dislike of cemeteries and monuments. I once saw Father very troubled and upset—an extremely rare occurrence. It was in Minsk, when he received news of the death of one of his hunting friends, a poor clerk; I never did know his name. I remember him as a tall man, with a bald patch and colourless eyes, shabbily dressed. He would always grow uncommonly animated talking of partridges, hares and quails; he preferred small game.

"A wolf—now, that isn't hunting, Sergei Alexandrovich," he would tell Father forcefully. "That's child's play. Wolves and bears are child's play."

"Whatever do you mean, child's play?" Father would say indignantly. "And elk? Wild boar? Would you even know a boar if you saw one?"

"I daresay I wouldn't, Sergei Alexandrovich. But all the same, as I've said, you won't change my mind."

"Well, have it your way." Father unexpectedly calmed down. "And do you also hold tea to be child's play?"

"No, Sergei Alexandrovich."

"Well then, let's have some tea. Seeing as it's only ever small beers you deal in, let's see how much tea you can drink."

This clerk and the artist Sipovsky were fixtures at our home in Minsk. Sipovsky was a tall old boy with a cross-looking brow, a keeper of borzois and a lover of art. He was colossal and broad-shouldered; his pockets were conspicuous for their terrible depth. Once, having come to visit us and finding no one save Nanny and me at home, he fixed me in his steady gaze and abruptly asked:

"Ever seen a rooster?"

"Yes."

"You aren't afraid of them?"

"No."

"Watch this."

He reached into his pocket and pulled out an enormous live rooster. The bird began scratching its claws on the floor and making circles around the hallway.

"Why do you have a rooster?" I asked.

"I'm going to draw it."

"But he won't stand still."

"I'll make him."

"No, you won't."

"Oh, yes, I will."

We went through to the nursery. Flailing her arms, Nanny shooed the rooster into the room. Holding it with one hand, Sipovsky drew with the other a chalk circle on the floor around it—and, after lurching a couple of times, the rooster, much to my amazement, stood still. Sipovsky sketched it quickly. I recall yet another of his drawings: a hunter, leaning to one side, astride a galloping horse;

directly in front of him, two borzois pressing on a wolf. The hunter's face was red and desperate; all four of the horse's legs were somehow interwoven together. Sipovsky made me a gift of the picture. I adored any illustration of an animal and knew, without ever having seen them, a great many species of wild beasts; what was more, I had read all three volumes of Brehm from cover to cover twice over. Once, while I was reading the second volume of *The Life of Animals*, Father's bitch, an English setter, gave birth to a litter. Father gave the blind little pups away to an acquaintance and left himself with a single puppy, the biggest. One evening, around three days later, the clerk paid us a visit.

"Sergei Alexandrovich," he said with tears in his voice, without so much as a word of greeting, "have you given away all the pups? Didn't you spare a thought for me?"

"I didn't," replied Father, his eyes fixed on the floor in embarrassment.

"So there isn't a single one left?"

"There's one, but he's mine."

"Give him to me, Sergei Alexandrovich."

"I cannot."

"Sergei Alexandrovich," said the clerk despairingly, "I'm an honest man. But if you won't give me the puppy, I'll have no choice but to steal it."

"Go ahead and try."

"And if I manage to steal it, without your noticing?"

"Then you're in luck."

"You won't ask for it back?"

"I shan't."

When he left, Father laughed and said in delight:

"Now there's a huntsman for you. That's the sort of talk I can understand."

He was well contented, and when several days later the pup did disappear, he made a great show of losing his temper and even said that apparently one couldn't keep anything safe at home—Nanny bolstered him unexpectedly, saying: today it's a dog, tomorrow it'll be the samovar they steal—and my sister, who was uncommonly curious, asked Mother: and then the piano, right, Mama? But the pup's disappearance clearly didn't aggrieve him in the least. The clerk didn't show his face for a couple of weeks, but he did turn up later. "How's the dog?" Father asked. The clerk just smiled broadly, without giving a word of reply. That pup grew remarkably fast. He was called Treasure, and very often when the clerk came to visit us Treasure would come bounding up behind him; we considered him almost a part of the family. Once—it was a sunny autumn day, Father had gone off somewhere and Mother was reading in her room—Treasure darted out from behind a corner, panting, his muzzle bloodied; he rushed up to me, started whining, tugged on my trouser leg and dragged me off with him. I went running after him. We passed through the Jewish quarter on the outskirts of the city and into the fields beyond the city limits, and there I saw the clerk lying motionless, face-down on the grass. I prodded him, called his name, peered into his face, but he just lay there. Treasure licked his head, which was encrusted with the blood that had trickled down his disfigured bald patch. The dog sat on its hind legs and began to howl; it would gasp from the howling and whine, and then it would begin howling again. A terribly eerie feeling gripped me. The three of us were alone in the field, there was a light breeze blowing in from the river; a fearsome antique rifle lay alongside the clerk's body. I don't recall how I managed to run all the way home. As soon as I saw Father, I told him everything. He frowned and, without so much as a word, galloped off; he had not even had time to unsaddle the horse, for he had only just arrived home. He returned twenty minutes later and explained that the clerk, while clumsily trying to discharge his rifle, had fired a whole buckshot cartridge straight into his forehead. Father was beside himself for several days, neither joked nor laughed, nor did he even caress me.

At mealtimes he would suddenly stop eating and lose himself in thought.

"What are you thinking about?" Mother would ask.

"It's such a preposterous thing!" he would say. "What a foolish way to die! Now he's gone—and there's not a thing to be done about it."

Only after some time did he regain his old self and each evening, as he always did, tell the continuation of our never-ending fairy tale: the story of how our whole family voyaged on board a ship that I commanded.

"We won't take Mother with us, Kolya," he would say. "She's afraid of the sea and will only upset the brave seafarers."

"Mama can stay at home," I agreed.

"So then, you and I are sailing across the Indian Ocean. Suddenly a storm gets up. You're the captain, everyone turns to you, awaiting their orders. You calmly give the command. What's it to be, Kolya?"

"Lower the lifeboats!" I shouted.

"Now, hang on, it's a bit early to go lowering the lifeboats. You say: furl the sails and don't be afraid."

"And they furl the sails," I continued.

"Yes, Kolya, they furl the sails."

Over the course of my childhood I had made several circumnavigations of the globe, discovered a new island, become its ruler, built a railroad across the sea and brought Mama directly to my island in a railway carriage—because Mama was terribly afraid of the sea and was not in the least ashamed to admit it. I grew so accustomed to hearing this fairy tale about our sea voyage every night that when every once in a while something would interrupt it—if Father was out of town, for example—I would be distressed almost to the point of tears. But afterwards, sitting on Father's knees and glancing from time to time at Mother's placid face—for she was usually by his side—I experienced true happiness, the sort that only a child or a man possessed of extraordinary spiritual strength can feel. Later, however, the fairy tale ended once and for all: my father fell ill and died.

Before his death he would say, gasping for breath:

"Only, please, just bury me without any priests or church rites."

But he was buried by a priest all the same: the bells that he so disliked tolled, and in the peaceful cemetery tall weeds grew wild. I kissed the waxen forehead; I was accompanied to the coffin, and my uncle lifted me up since I was too small. That moment when, dangling awkwardly in my uncle's hands, I peered into the coffin and saw Father's black beard, moustache and closed eyes was the most terrifying moment of my life. The high vaults of the church hummed, aunts' dresses rustled, and all of a sudden I saw the inhuman, hardened face of my mother. In that fleeting instant I understood everything: an icy feeling of death gripped me, and I succumbed to a morbid delirium, having all at once espied my own end somewhere in the infinite distance—that same fate as my father's. I should have been glad to die in that very instant, to share in Father's lot and be together with him. Everything darkened before my eyes. I was brought over to Mother, and her cold hand came to rest atop my head; I looked up at her, but she neither saw me nor knew that I was standing beside her. We returned home from the cemetery directly; the carriage bobbed up and down on its springs, my father's grave was left behind, the wind danced before me. Further and further on, the horses' backs silently glide; we arrive home, but Father lies there motionless; I've perished with him, and so too my fabulous ship, and the island with the white buildings which I discovered in the Indian Ocean. The air trembled before my eyes; all of a sudden a yellow light flashed ahead of me, an awe-inspiring, bright flame; the blood rushed to my head and I felt dreadful. At home I was put to bed; I had diphtheria.

———

The Indian Ocean, a yellow sky above the sea, a black boat slowly cleaving the water. I stand on the bridge, pink birds fly over the stern, and the burning, torrid air rings quietly. I'm sailing aboard my pirate ship, but I'm sailing alone. Where, oh where, is Father? Just then the ship passes along a tree-lined shore; through my telescope I spy among the branches the fleeting figure of Mother's great ambler and behind it, at a broad, sweeping trot, Father's black racer. We hoist sail and for a long time sail on, keeping pace with the horses. Suddenly Father turns to me. "Papa, where are you going?" I cry. And his muffled, distant voice answers something unintelligible. "Where?" I ask again. "Captain," the master says to me, "this man's being taken to the cemetery." Sure enough, the empty hearse is travelling along the yellow road without a driver, and the white coffin is gleaming in the sun. "Papa is dead!" I cry. Mother leans over me. Her hair is loose, her cold face terrible and stony.

"No, Kolya, Papa isn't dead."

"Furl the sails and don't be afraid," I command. "A storm's gathering!"

"He's screaming again," says Nanny.

But now we are crossing the Indian Ocean, and we drop anchor. Everything sinks into darkness: the sailors are asleep, the white coastal town is asleep, my father sleeps in a profound blackness, somewhere not far from me, and just then, the black sails of the *Flying Dutchman* sweep heavily past our slumbering boat.

Some while later I began to recover; Nanny would sit for hours at my bedside, telling me all manner of things—I learnt a great deal from her. She told me that in Siberia they sold frozen cakes of milk in the street, that at night they would leave out food on the windowsill for fugitive convicts who would roam, all the bitter winter, the towns and villages. According to Nanny, my parents' life in Siberia had been marvellous.

"The mistress didn't know the first thing about house-keeping," Nanny would say. "Not a thing. Couldn't tell a chicken from a duck. We had a lot of chickens, only none of them laid eggs. We had to buy eggs at market. They were cheap, those eggs, thirty-five copecks for a hundred, not like what it is here. Two copecks for a pound of meat. And they sold butter by the barrel. But the housekeeper was a sly one. One time, the late master was going down the street and an old woman comes up to him:

"'You wouldn't know where I can find the forester's house, would you?' she says. That was to say, ours. The master says: 'I would indeed. And whom do you wish to see?' 'Their housekeeper,' she says. 'She's selling eggs ever so cheaply—it's cheaper than at the market.' So they set off shopping together, the old woman in front and the master behind. Well, the housekeeper confessed everything. She cried and cried. Oh, she was a sorry sight."

"Tell me about Vasilyevna, Nanny!"

"Now I'll tell you about Vasilyevna. The mistress took on a cook. Oh, she was a stern-looking woman, about fifty, or perhaps thirty."

"But Nanny, that's a big difference."

"It most certainly is not," said Nanny with conviction. "Now you listen to me or I shan't tell you the story."

"All right, I'll be good."

"She was called Vasilyevna. 'I'm not from these parts,' she says. 'Only my son's doing hard labour. I'm from Petersburg myself. I can cook anything,' she says. And true enough, so she could. Life went on, and then one day the mistress invited some guests round. Vasilyevna was to make a pie, and the table was laid that afternoon. In the evening the mistress arrives home, on horseback, as she always did—a lovely horse it was, a bay. We didn't normally keep bays, but it was lovely all the same. So in she comes and sees: nothing, not a thing, the place is bare. No pie, dishes scattered everywhere. She goes to the kitchen. And Vasilyevna's sitting there, all red-faced and fierce-looking, God preserve us! The mistress asks why nothing's ready. 'What's got into you, Vasilyevna?'

she says. Then the woman replies: 'I'm a lady myself, so don't you shout at me. I won't serve any more; I want to eat too.' And sure enough, the pie had been nibbled all over. Then Vasilyevna ran out of the house and only on the sixth day did she return. She came back filthy, ragged, her dress torn all over, herself in tears. 'Forgive me,' she says, 'I have these terrible drinking bouts and there isn't a thing to be done about it.' Quite the puritan."

"Who is, Nanny?"

"A puritan? Vasilyevna. Now you go to sleep, and your illness will nod off, too. And later it will pass. Sleep now."

It was an airy, gossamer day when I went outside for the first time. Little white clouds were racing away, but already in the east the chill air showed blue. I thought that it must have been on such a day that Andersen's field mouse, while sheltering Thumbelina, bolted the door to his hole, inspected the stock of grain, and in the evening, as he lay down to sleep, said: "Well, now all that's left is to arrange the wedding. You ought to thank the good Lord; after all, it isn't every bridegroom that has a fur coat like a mole's. And, don't let's forget, you haven't any dowry, if you please."

I felt deeply sorry for Thumbelina, and sympathized especially with her loneliness—for I had spent my entire childhood alone. For all that, though, I never shunned my peers. I played at soldiers, hide-and-seek, and was, in the estimations of many, even too boisterous; yet I never loved any of them, and without sorrow or regret I would part with those from whom circumstance separated me. I grew used to people quickly and, having done so, I would cease to mark their existence. This was, I suppose, a love of solitude, but a rather curious, elaborate form of it. Whenever I found myself alone, I would always want to pin my ears to something; others prevented me from doing this. I cared nothing for confidences, but since I had a knack for quick imagination, heart-to-heart talks came easily to me. While I never lied, nor did I express the full extent of my thoughts; thus, unwittingly, did I discharge myself of the burden of candid declarations. I had no friends. Later I realized that I had been wrong to act like this. I paid dearly for the mistake: I deprived myself of one of life's most valuable opportunities. I understood the words "friend" and "pal" only in theory, although I made incredible efforts to confect a feeling of friendship within myself. Yet I managed to achieve only an abstract under-standing of it, a sense of others' friendship. But one day, all of a sudden, I grasped it to the core; it became especially precious when the spectre of death or old age appeared, when so much of what had been acquired together was then lost together. I thought: friendship—it means that we're still alive while others have died. I remember having a friend called Dikov while I was at the military academy; we became friends because we were both good at walking on our hands. We never saw each other again after I was taken out of the academy. I remembered Dikov just as I did all the others—which is to say, I never thought about him. Many years later, one torrid day at Sebastopol, I saw at the cemetery a wooden cross and a nameplate with the inscription "Here lies Cadet Dikov, Timofeyevo Academy, who died of typhus". In that moment I felt as if I had lost a friend. God knows why this stranger had become so dear to me, as if I had spent my whole life with him. I noticed then that this feeling of loss and sorrow grows particularly strong on beautiful days, particularly when the air is clear and limpid. It struck me that equivalent states existed also within my soul, and that if somewhere deep within me there fell a silence replacing the gentle, incessant rush of my spiritual life, a rush that I hardly ever heard but which was always present and weakened only slightly in certain moments, then it would mean that some great catastrophe had occurred. And I would imagine a vast expanse of land, as flat as the desert and visible to its very end, its remote edge suddenly broken by a deep crevice, silently falling into an abyss and carrying away everything with it. A silence descends. Then, without a sound, a second layer breaks away, and then a third, and so on until all that remains is but a few steps separating me from the edge; and finally my legs sink into the burning sand; and in a slow-moving cloud of sand I sail heavily down, in the wake of everything else that has already gone before me. Just above my head a yellow light burns, and the sun, like a colossal lantern, lights up the black water of a still lake and a deathly orange land. I feel wretched—and, as always, begin to think of Mother, whom I knew less well than Father and who forever remained a mystery to me. She was not at all like Father—not in her habits, in her tastes, nor in her character. It seemed to me as though she harboured within her the same potential for internal rupture, the same threat of an irrevocably split personality that unquestionably existed within me. Very tranquil in nature, somewhat chilly in demeanour, she never raised her voice. Petersburg, where she had lived until her marriage, Grandmother's sedate house, governesses, scoldings and the mandatory reading of classic authors had all left their mark on her. The maidservant—who wasn't afraid of Father even when he shouted in his booming voice: the Devil knows what nonsense this is!—always feared Mother, who spoke slowly and never lost her temper. From the earliest days of my childhood, I can remember her unhurried movements, the coldness that emanated from her and her well-bred smile; she hardly ever laughed. She rarely caressed her children, and while I would come running to Father and leap up onto his chest—knowing full well that this strong man only occasionally pretended to be an adult, whereas in actual fact he and I were of the same age, and that if I were to invite him there and then to come out into the garden and pull me in my toy carriages, he would think about it and then go—I approached Mother quietly, decorously, as befitted a well-brought-up boy, and naturally wouldn't allow myself to shout with glee or go tearing into the parlour. I didn't fear Mother: no one in our house was punished—not I, nor my sisters. Yet I could never shake off that feeling of her superiority over me, one that was inexplicable though undeniable. In no measure did it depend on her knowledge or her abilities, which truly were exceptional. Her memory was altogether infallible: she remembered everything that she ever heard or read. She spoke French and German with irreproachable precision and an exactitude that may well have sounded too classical; but even in her Russian speech, my mother—for all her lack of affectation and aversion to flamboyant expressions—used only literary turns and spoke with her customary chilliness and intonations of indifference that bordered on the scornful. Such had she always been. Only for Father would she suddenly break into an exuberantly joyful smile from across the table or in the parlour—something that I never saw her do under any other circumstances. She often reprimanded me, with absolute equanimity, uttering the words in that same even tone of voice, whereupon my father would cast me a sympathetic look and, with a nod of his head, lend me some tacit support. Then he would say:

"Let him be. He won't do it again. Will you, Kolya?"

"No, Papa."

"Well, run along then."

I would turn to go, and he would observe with an apologetic tone:

"At the end of the day, it would be a worry if he was quiet and didn't play up. Still waters run deep."

When admonishing me and explaining why one ought to act in one way and not another, Mother almost never engaged in discussion with me—which is to say, she did not allow for the possibility that I might contradict her. With Father I argued, with Mother—never. I remember once trying to answer back; she regarded me with astonishment and curiosity, as though noticing for the first time that I possessed the gift of speech. But then, I was the least capable member of the family: my sisters took after Mother entirely in their quick understanding and prodigious memory, and they developed more rapidly than

I did; I was never made to comprehend this, although I knew it well enough myself. In childhood, just as later on, I was a stranger to envy, and I loved my mother dearly despite her chilliness. This placid woman, who was like the embodiment of a painting and seemed to preserve within herself its marvellous stillness, was in fact not at all what she seemed. It took me years to understand this, but, having understood, I would sit for long hours lost in meditation, imagining her true and not her seeming life. She adored literature so much that it was odd. She would read often and voraciously and, having finished a book, would refuse to talk or answer any of my questions; she would stare straight ahead with unmoving, unseeing eyes and notice nothing around her. She knew by heart so very many poems, the whole of Lermontov's *Daemon*, all of Pushkin's *Eugene Onegin*, from the first line to the last; however, she cared little for Father's reading tastes—nothing was of less interest to her than German philosophy or sociology. Never in our house did I see fashionable novels, Verbitskaya or Artsybashev; both Father and Mother ostensibly saw eye to eye in their unanimous scorn for them. It was I who brought the first such book into the house; Father was no longer alive by then, and I was in my fourth year at the gymnasium. The book, which I had accidentally left in the dining room, was Artsybashev's

A Woman Standing in the Middle. Mother happened to see it—and when I returned home that evening, she asked me, wincingly lifting the title page of the book between two fingers:

"Is this reading matter yours? What fine taste you have."

I could have wept with shame, and for evermore afterwards the recollection that Mother knew of my short-lived predilection for pornographic and frivolous novels was for me a most humiliating memory. Had she been able to tell my father, I doubt I should have survived the blow.

Mother loved my father with all her strength, with all her soul. She didn't cry when he died, and both Nanny and I were terrified of being left alone with her. For three months, from early morning until late at night, she would pace incessantly about the parlour from one corner to another. She spoke with no one, scarcely ate, slept only three or four hours a night and never went out. Our relatives were sure that she was losing her mind. I remember how at night I would wake up in the nursery and hear the quick patter of her feet across the carpet; I would fall asleep, waken—and again: that same barely audible squeak of slippers and Mother's rapid footsteps. I would get out of bed and in my bare feet and nightshirt go into the parlour.

"Mama, go to bed. Mama, why are you always walking around?"

Mama would look straight at me: I would see her pale, estranged face and terrifying eyes.

"Mama, I'm scared. Mama, lie down for a little while."

She would sigh, as though waking from a trance.

"Very well, Kolya, I'll lie down. Go to sleep."

In the beginning, my mother's life had been a happy one. Father devoted all his time to the family, freeing himself only for hunting and scientific work—nothing else interested him. He was exceedingly gallant with ladies, never argued with them and agreed even when they said something utterly at odds with his own views—but more generally he failed to see the reason for women on this earth. Mother would say to him:

"You called Vera Mikhaylovna 'Vera Vladimirovna' again. She'll doubtless have taken offence. How is it that you still can't remember? She's been visiting us for almost two years now."

"Yes?" Father marvelled. "Which one is she? The wife of the engineer who whistles?"

"No, Daria Vasilyevna's the one who whistles; the engineer sings. None of which has anything to do with Vera Mikhaylovna. She's the wife of the doctor, Sergei Ivanovich."

"Why, of course." Father grew animated. "I know her perfectly well."

"Yes, but you call her Vera Vasilyevna one day and Vera Petrovna the next. Her name is Vera Mikhaylovna."

"Astonishing," Father would say. "*Mea culpa*. Now I remember quite clearly. I know this lady perfectly well. As I recall, she's terribly sweet. And her husband's a nice chap. Though their pointer isn't much to write home about."

There were never any disagreements or quarrels at home; things ran smoothly. But fate did not indulge Mother for long. First my elder sister died; her death occurred when she took a bath too soon following an operation on her stomach. Then, several years later, Father died, and finally, during the Great War, my younger sister, who was only nine years old at the time, died of fulminant scarlet fever, after taking ill for only a couple of days. After that, there was only Mother and I. She lived a rather secluded life; I was left to my own devices and did freely as I pleased. She could never forget the losses that had befallen her so unexpectedly and spent long years as though under a spell, even more silent and still than before. She enjoyed remarkable good health and was never ill, and only her eyes, which I remembered as bright and aloof, betrayed a grief so profound that, whenever I looked at them, I felt ashamed for myself and for the fact that I still lived upon this earth. Later on, my mother and I grew closer somehow, and I came to know the extraordinary strength of her love for the memory of my father and sisters, and her mournful love for me. I also came to know that she had been endowed with a supple and quick imagination that surpassed my own significantly and an ability to understand such things that I should never have suspected. Indeed, her superiority, which I had sensed since childhood, was only further confirmed to me as I neared adulthood. And there was something else that I came to understand, something of the utmost importance: that the world of my secondary existence, which I had thought to be closed forever and to everyone, was known to my mother.

I was separated from Mother for the first time when I became a cadet. The academy was located in another city, and I remember the blue-and-white river, the green treetops of Timofeyevo, and the hotel where Mother brought me two weeks before my entrance exams and where she went through a little French grammar with me. (I had trouble with spelling.) Then came the examination, farewell to Mother, a new uniform and a tunic with epaulettes, and a cabby in a torn peasant coat, who tugged on the reins so mercilessly and bore Mother down to the railway station, from where the train carried her home. And so I was left alone.

I kept my distance from the other cadets, spent hours wandering through the echoing halls of the academy and only later realized that I had far-off Christmas and a fortnight's holiday to look forward to. I didn't like the academy. My peers differed from me in many respects: they were, in the majority of cases, the children of officers and came from a semi-military background that I had never known. No military types had ever visited us; Father had always regarded them with hostility and disdain. I could never accustom myself to the "yes, sir" and "no, sir", and I recall once having replied to a dressing-down from an officer: you're partly right, Colonel, sir—for which I was punished further still. Then again, I soon made friends with the other cadets; the top brass never did like me, although I was a good student. The methods of instruction at the academy were of the most diverse nature. One German would try to make the whole class read aloud in unison, and so amid the text of our German reader one could always discern cocks crowing, bawdy songs and all manner of shrieking. The teachers were third-rate: not one of them distinguished himself in any way, with the exception of our natural history teacher, a civilian general, a wry old boy, a materialist and a sceptic.

"What is hygroscopic wadding, Your Excellency?"

And he would answer:

"Say a young cadet such as yourself were to go running around the courtyard and jump about like a calf, accidentally cutting his tail off—well, they'd apply the wadding to the wound. They do this so that the cadet resembling a calf isn't too put out. Understood?"

"Yes, sir, Your Excellency."

"Yes, sir..." he would mumble, smiling gloomily. "I despair..."

I don't know why I found this civilian general so utterly delightful, but whenever he turned his attention to me, I was very glad of it. Once, I was called on to recite a lesson that I knew well, and several times I used the words "foremost", "primarily" and "essentially". He looked at me with a cheerful smirk and awarded me a good mark.

"What an erudite cadet. 'Foremost' and 'essentially'. Essentially, you may sit down."

Another time he stopped me in the corridor, pulled a serious face and said:

"I would ask you, Cadet Sosedov, not to waggle your behind around quite so much when you walk. It only attracts attention."

With that, he walked off, smiling with his eyes alone. He was a one-off, quite unlike any of the other teachers at the academy. In fact, the only thing I learnt there was the art of walking on my hands. And later, a long time after I left the academy, whenever I had occasion to stand on my hands, I would immediately see in front of me the waxed parquet of the recreational hall, dozens of legs walking alongside my arms, and the beard of my form tutor:

"No pudding for you today again, sonny."

He always used diminutives when talking, and this provoked in me an indomitable feeling of revulsion. I didn't like people who used diminutives in an ironic way: there is nothing more petty or base in a language. I noticed that it was most often those lacking in culture who had recourse to such expressions, or else they were simply wicked, villains invariably on the lowest rungs of humanity. The presence of my form tutor was unpleasant in itself. But what I found particularly stifling about the academy was that I couldn't lose my temper all of a sudden and go home: home was far away, in another city, a whole day's journey by railway. Winter, the enormous dark academy building, the long, dimly lit corridors, the loneliness: it oppressed and bored me. I lacked the inclination to study, and lying in bed was forbidden me. We cadets whiled away the time "ice-skating" down the freshly waxed parquet; we left the tap on in the washroom all night long, leapt over chairs and lecterns, and placed countless bets on the rissoles, puddings, sugar and macaroni. We were all of us rather mediocre students, with the exception of Uspensky, who was top of our class and the most diligent and unhappy cadet in our company. He would swot frenziedly and prepare lessons from dinner until nine in the evening, when we went to bed. He would spend an hour and a half on his knees in prayer every night, sobbing silently. Being the son of very poor parents, he studied at the state's expense and so had to achieve consistently high marks.

"What are you praying for, Uspensky?" I would ask, waking up and seeing a figure in a long nightshirt in front of a little icon on top of his pillow: he slept two beds along from me.

"I'm praying for my studies," he quickly replied in his usual tone of voice, before immediately continuing in a frenzy:

"Our Father which art in heaven…" Except he understood the words of the prayer poorly and spoke the words "which art" as though they meant "seeing as you're up there".

"You're not saying it properly, Uspensky," I would tell him. "'Our Father which art in heaven'—you have to say it all in one go."

He would suddenly break off his prayer and begin to cry.

"What's the matter with you?"

"Why don't you just leave me alone?"

"Fine, I will. Pray then, be my guest."

And once again the silence, the beds, the smoking night lamps, darkness beneath the ceiling and a little white figure on its knees. Then in the morning the drum would thunder, the bugle would bray through the wall, and the duty officer would pass along the rows of beds:

"Reveille, get up!"

I never could quite get used to the military official-ese. At home we spoke pure and correct Russian, and so the language of the academy set my teeth on edge. I once happened to see the company log, which bore the following inscription: "So much fabric distributed for the purposes of fabricating tunics", and further down there was an entry about expenses for the "glassing" of windows. I discussed these turns of phrase with two of my comrades and we decided that the duty officer—for we were convinced that it was he who had written them—was illiterate. Of course, this was not at all far from the truth, although we scarcely knew the officer who was on duty that day: all we knew was that he was a man of devout faith. The academy took the matter of religion very seriously: we were taken to church every Saturday and Sunday, and it was to this inescapable procession that I owed my subsequent hatred of the Orthodox service. Everything about it seemed loath-some to me: from the greasy hair of the fat deacon, who only after blowing his nose loudly at the altar, quickly tweaking his nose and clearing his throat with a short cough, would commence the service and in his deep bass bellow: bless us, O Lord!—to the priest and his absurd, weedy voice, which would reply from behind the closed sanctuary doors that were plastered in gilt, icons and daubs of chubby-legged angels with melancholy faces and thick lips:

"Blessed is the kingdom of the Father, and of the Son, and of the Holy Ghost, as it was in the beginning, is now and ever shall be: world without end…"

And so too the long-legged cantor with a tuning fork, who himself sang as he listened to the singing of others, which imbued his face with a look of incredible tension; all this seemed absurd and unnecessary to me, although I didn't always comprehend why. Yet as I studied the Scripture and read the Gospels, I would think:

"What sort of a Christian is our lieutenant colonel? He doesn't observe a single one of the commandments; he's forever punishing me, making me stand in the corner, making me go without pudding. Is that really Christ's teaching?"

I turned to Uspensky, a recognized expert on matters of Scripture.

"What do you think?" I asked. "Is our lieutenant colonel a Christian?"

"Of course he is," he said quickly and in alarm.

"Then what right does he have to punish me almost every day?"

"Because you don't behave yourself."

"Yes, but in the Gospel is it not said: judge not, that ye be not judged?"

"Be not judged, that's the passive voice," Uspensky whispered to himself, as though testing his knowledge. "He wasn't talking about a cadet."

"Then who was he talking about?"

"I don't know."

"So you don't understand the Scripture," I said, turning to leave. And so my hostility in respect of both religion and the academy was only strengthened further.

Much later, when I was a student at the gymnasium, I remembered the military academy as though it were a heavy, leaden dream. It lived on somewhere deep inside me. I recalled particularly the smell of wax on the parquet and the taste of rissoles and macaroni, and the moment

I heard anything that reminded me of it, immediately in my mind's eye I would see the enormous dark halls, the night lamps, the dormitory, the long nights and the morning drum, Uspensky in his white nightshirt, and the lieutenant colonel who was such a bad Christian. That life had been arduous and bleak, and I found my recollection of the academy's stony torpor repellent, like the memory of a barracks, or a prison, or a long sojourn in some godforsaken place, in some cold railway linesman's hut somewhere between Moscow and Smolensk, lost in the snow, in a deserted, frosty wilderness.

And yet, the early years of my schooling were the most unclouded, happiest years of my life. In the beginning—both at the academy and at the gymnasium I later attended—I was bewildered by the sheer number of my classmates. I didn't know how to talk to all these neatly shorn boys. I was used to having several lives around me: Mother's, my sisters' and Nanny's—ones that were dear and familiar to me—but such a mass of new and strange people could not be taken in at once. I was afraid that I might lose myself in the crowd, and my instinct for self-preservation, which usually lay dormant, was suddenly roused and provoked a host of changes in my nature, which, in any other circumstances, would likely not have taken place. I would often find myself saying things that were not at all what I thought, and I didn't act as one ought: I grew impudent, cast off that sluggishness of action and reaction that since Father's death had reigned unchallenged in our home as though it were spellbound by Mother's frigid magic. I found it difficult to break my school habits at home, although I mastered the art before long. I knew instinctively that one couldn't be the same with everyone, and so, after a brief period of minor domestic wrangling, I once again settled down into my role as the obedient boy in the family; at school, however, my sharp tongue was the reason that I was punished more than others. Despite my being the least capable member of the family, I had nevertheless partly inherited Mother's good memory, although I was never wholly aware of it and would understand the full significance of what was explained to me only some time after the event. Father's gifts were transmitted to me in a much-altered form: rather than his strength of will and patience, I was endowed with stubbornness; rather than his hunting prowess—his sharp sight, physical indefatigability and keen powers of observation—I inherited only an unusual, blind love for the animal kingdom and an intense though unwitting and aimless interest in everything that went on around me, everything that was said and done. I was a reluctant student, although I received decent enough marks; it was only my behaviour that provoked discussions in staff meetings. This was due in part to the fact that I had never experienced that childish fear of teachers, nor did I ever hide my feelings towards them. My form tutor complained to Mother that I was ill-mannered and impudent, though almost exceptionally advanced for my age. Mother, who was often called to the gymnasium, would say:

"Forgive me, but I do not believe that you have quite mastered the art of dealing with children. At home Kolya is a very quiet boy and not at all a troublemaker. He never usually answers back."

She then sent the servitor to fetch me. I walked into the office and greeted her; having spoken with me for ten minutes, she dismissed me.

"Yes, he takes an entirely different tone with you," the form tutor admitted. "I don't know how you do it. He's simply unbearable in class." He folded his arms in indignation. The impudence that I showed our history master provoked the opprobrium of both my form tutor and the proctor. One day the following conversation took place: "Who was Konrad Wallenrod?" I asked, having read the name in a book and failed to recognize it. After pausing to think, the history master replied: "He was a hooligan, just like you"—after which he made me stand facing the wall for "not sitting still". I was hardly at fault: my neighbour had drawn his rubber across my forehead (something the teacher did not see), for which I punched him in the chest (something he did see). Since I couldn't rat on my classmate, I said nothing to the historian's words: stand facing the wall if you're unable to conduct yourself decently. The historian, by then used to my constant objections and this time not hearing them, suddenly lost his temper, exploded, banged his chair on the floor, but, making a false move, tripped and fell over beside the lectern. The class did not dare to laugh.

"Serves you right," I said.

He was beside himself with rage, ordered me out of the classroom and told me to go and see the proctor. But later, since he was a good man, he calmed down and forgave me, though I had not asked his forgiveness. On the whole he treated me without malice; my chief adversary was my form tutor, the Russian master, who hated me as people do their equal. Of course, he could not give me poor marks, because I knew Russian better than the others. But still, I would "go without lunch" almost every day. I remember the infinitely miserable feeling with which I would look on as everyone left to go home after the fifth lesson; the first to go would be those who packed away their things quickly, then others, then finally the slowest, while I would be left alone, gazing at a mysterious blank map that recalled the lunar landscapes in my father's books. The blackboard would be adorned with a cambric duster and a monstrous little devil that Paramonov, the class artist, had drawn; and for some reason that little devil would remind me of the artist Sipovsky. This state of tedium would continue for around an hour until the form tutor arrived:

"Go home and try to conduct yourself less like a hooligan in future."

At home dinner and books awaited me, and in the evening playing in the courtyard, where I was not supposed to go. At the time we were living in a building that belonged to Alexei Vasilyevich Voronin, a former officer of good noble lineage, a strange and remarkable man. He was tall, wore thick moustaches and a beard that seemed to hide his face; his bright, angry eyes, I recall, always unsettled me. For some reason, I thought this man knew things about me that should never be told. He was fearsome in his rages, inclined to forget himself, capable of shooting anyone: the long months during the siege of Port Arthur had left their mark on his nervous system. He produced the impression of a man who carried within himself a silent strength. But for all that, he was a kind man, although he spoke to children with an invariably harsh tone, was never affected by them and never used affectionate names for them. He was clever and well educated and possessed the skill to grasp abstract ideas and unfamiliar feelings—something one hardly ever sees in ordinary people. This man understood far more than was necessary for a retired officer to live out his life. He had a son, who was four or so years older than me, and two daughters, Marianna and Natalia, one of whom was my age, the other ages with my sister. Alexei Vasilyevich's wife, a German by birth and a perennial advocate of wrongdoers, was well known for her inability to turn down any request made of her. One would say to her:

"Ekaterina Heinrichovna, I couldn't trouble you for some bread and jam, could I? You know, the one you made for New Year's?"

"Heavens above, dearie!" she would say, horrified. "I mustn't touch that jam."

"But Ekaterina Heinrichovna, I'd be ever so grateful. Couldn't you find a way?"

"Oh, what a funny thing you are. Well, I'll have to give you a different jam, an English one, but it's also very tasty…"

"No, Ekaterina Heinrichovna, I know that one's no good. It smells of tar. Can't I have the one for New Year's?"

"You don't understand the simplest things… Oh, very well then, give me your bread here and I'll fetch it for you."

In her veins flowed such stalwart and healthy blood that over the long years she didn't change and was seemingly impervious to ageing: she had reached the age of twenty-five and remained so for the rest of her life. Under no circumstances did she lose her constant, calm, fussing nature, nor did she ever forget anything or get worked up. When a fire broke out in the courtyard one night—the woodshed had caught fire—and I woke up because all around was brightly lit by the flames and my windowpane was cracking from the heat, I saw Ekaterina Heinrichovna standing at my bedside, dressed just as she would have been had it happened in the light of day, calm and not a hair out of place.

"I didn't want to wake you," she said. "You were sleeping so peacefully, but you'd better get up just in case, God forbid, the house should catch fire. Only mind not to fall asleep again. I still have to go and wake your mother. This is what comes of people who don't take care with fire."

At the time her son was a fourth-year pupil at the gymnasium, a very kind sort, but wayward and unstable. My mother didn't care for his piano playing. He did possess certain musical abilities, but he pounded on the keyboard with such ferocity and worked the pedals so unforgivingly that she would say:

"Misha, why are you wasting so much energy?"

To which he would reply:

"Because I get so carried away."

We nicknamed the Voronins' younger daughter "Sophie", since she was so like the young heroine of a book we had read—*Les Malheurs de Sophie*. This girl cultivated a love of unusual adventures. She would dash off to the bazaar and spend all day there wandering around among the traders, pickpockets and even bigger thieves (men in good suits with wide-legged trousers), knife-grinders, booksellers, butchers and those purveyors of junk who seemingly exist in every city on the globe, who are clad identically in black rags and are pidgin-speakers of every language, flogging the sort of flotsam that not a soul needs; and yet they live on, and in their families one generation gives way to the next, as if fate itself had foreordained them to no other trade but this—in my eyes they personified a magnificent immutability. Or else she would take off her stockings and slippers and go barefoot about the garden after the rain had passed and, having returned home, boast:

"Mama, just look how black my feet are."

"Your feet certainly are very black," Ekaterina Heinrichovna would answer. "Only, what's so good about that?"

The elder daughter, Marianna, was known for her reserve, her precocious femininity and her prodigious strength of character. Once, when she was eleven years old, her father branded her an idiot: he was in one of his fits of rage, which caused him to forgo his usual civility. She paled and said:

"Now I won't talk to you."

And so for two years she didn't speak to him. She lorded it over her brother and sister, and her family was not so much afraid of her as they were wary. Each of the children was beautiful in a good, robust way; they were physically strong and inclined to gaiety, but, thanks to their mother's German blood, they were not the fully fledged Russian sanguine type.

The Voronin children and I constituted only a part of the assembly of youths that in the evenings would gather in the garden or in the courtyard of the Voronins' house. There were some other boys and girls who joined us: a beautiful little Jewish girl, Silva, who later became an actress; the twelve-year-old twins Valya and Lyalya, who were forever at each other's throats; and the realist Volodya, who would die of diphtheria ere long. While there was still light, we all played hopscotch; which is to say, we jumped about some squares drawn on the earth; these squares ended in a big, uneven circle that contained the word "heaven", and a little circle, "hell". As it grew dark, we would begin a game of hide and seek, and only after the maid had called us at least three times would we go our separate ways home. I divided my time between reading, school and the courtyard at home. There were long stretches of time when I would forget about that world of inner existence where I had once dwelt. Occasionally, however, I would return to it—this was usually heralded by a bout of illness, irritability and poor appetite—and I noticed that my second existence, endowed as it was with the capacity for innumerable metamorphoses and possibilities, was hostile to my first and gained in hostility as the first was enriched with new knowledge and strength. It was as if my second existence feared its own destruction, which would occur the moment that I reached my full physical potential. In those times I carried out bleak, silent work as I tried to attain a completeness and a union of these two disparate lives, much as I had done after I realized the necessity of being tough at school and placid at home. But that had been a simple affair; in this instance, I sensed that such efforts were beyond me. Besides which, I cherished my inner life more than others did. I noticed that in general my attention was more often attracted by subjects that should not have concerned me, while it remained indifferent to so much that affected me directly. Usually much time would have to pass before I could understand the true sense of a particular event, and only after it had completely lost its influence on my susceptibility would it acquire the significance it ought to have had to begin with. First it would migrate to a distant, illusory region, where my imagination would delve but rarely, and where I would find, as it were, the geological strata of my private history. Images that rose up before me would silently crumble, and again I would have to begin everything from scratch; only after the experience of a severe shock and having descended into the depths of consciousness would I discover there the debris in which I had once lived, the ruins of cities I had left behind. This absence of a direct, immediate response to anything that happened to me, this inability to know at once what to do, was later to become a source of profound unhappiness for me and the reason for the spiritual catastrophe that occurred soon after my first encounter with Claire. But that came a little later.

For a long time I was unable to comprehend my sudden bouts of fatigue—those days when I had done nothing and had no reason to be tired. As I lay down in bed, however, I would feel as though I had laboured for several hours straight. Later on, I surmised that those mysterious laws of internal motion were compelling me continually to seek and chase after whatever it was that would reveal itself to me only fleetingly in the guise of a colossal, shapeless mass, like some underwater monster—vanishing no sooner than it appeared. Physically this exhaustion manifested itself in headaches, and sometimes I would experience a strange pain in my eyes, as if someone were squashing them with his fingers. And not for a moment in the depths of my consciousness did this silent struggle cease, this struggle in which I myself played almost no role whatsoever. I would often lose myself: I was not something that had been defined once and for all; I changed, growing now bigger, now smaller; and perhaps it was this infidelity of my own spectre, one that would not allow me to split definitively into two separate beings, that permitted me in my real life to diversify more than would have seemed possible.

Those first unclouded years of my life at the gymnasium were seldom burdened by those inner crises from which I suffered so greatly and wherein I nevertheless found agonizing pleasure. I lived happily—if one can indeed live happily when an unrelenting shadow lurks behind one's shoulders. Death had never strayed far from me, and the abyss into which my imagination plunged me seemed to be his domain. I believe this feeling to have been hereditary: not for nothing was my father so violently averse to anything that reminded him of the inevitable; it was here that this fearless man had sensed his own impotence. My mother's cold, unconscious indifference was the true reflection of that final stillness, and her fervent memory of my sisters absorbed everything so rapidly because somewhere in its remote forebodings their deaths had already existed. Sometimes I dreamt that I was dead, that I was dying, that I was about to die; I could not cry out, and a familiar silence, which I had known so long, descended around me; it would suddenly expand and alter, taking on a new, hitherto unknown meaning: it was a warning to me.

My whole life—even when I was a child—I have felt as though I were in possession of some secret that others don't know; and this strange delusion has never left me. It couldn't have been based on external facts: I was no more or less educated than the rest of my untaught generation. It was a feeling independent of my own will. Very rarely, during the most intense moments of my life, I would experience a sort of momentary, almost physical transformation, and that is when I would draw nearer to my blind knowledge, to my illusory comprehension of the miraculous. But later I would return to my senses: I would sit there, pale and weak, and, just as before, everything around me would be lost in its stony, static form, and objects would resume the enduring, deceitful guise to which my sight had grown accustomed.

In the wake of such experiences, I would forget about them for a long while and return to my quotidian cares and, if it was summer, to my preparations for going away—for every year during the holidays I would go to the Caucasus, where my father's many relatives lived. There, from my grandfather's house, which stood on the outskirts of town, I would set out into the mountains. Eagles would soar high in the air, and I would walk through the tall grass with my Monte Cristo rifle, which I used to shoot sparrows and cats; alongside me the surging Terek roared, and a solitary black windmill rose up above its dirty waves. In the distance, on the mountains, snow shimmered—and once again I recalled the snowdrift that I had seen near Minsk so many years ago. On reaching the forest, I lay down near the first anthill I came across, caught a caterpillar and carefully placed it by one of the entrances to the tall, porous pyramid from which the ants came scurrying out. The caterpillar crawled away, coiling its hairy body into itself. It was overtaken by an ant; the ant caught on to its tail and tried to hold it back, but the caterpillar easily dragged the ant behind it. Others came scurrying to the aid of the first ant: they clung to the caterpillar on all sides, and the living ball slowly inched its way back before finally disappearing into one of the openings. It was the same fate that befell some large flies with blue wings, earthworms and even beetles, although these last were the most difficult for the ants to handle: the beetles were smooth and hard, and they were not easy to catch hold of. Yet the cruellest struggle I observed that day was when I placed a large black tarantula on the anthill. Never have I seen a fiercer creature—not among wild beasts or insects famed for their cruelty, if one can call thus their inscrutable instinct. The most cunning animals I had encountered—polecats, hamsters, weasels—generally possessed certain analytical faculties and in case of danger retreated, only attacking their enemy if there was no hope of escape. Only once did I see a weasel clinging to the hand of a groom that had wounded it with a stone: ordinarily, a weasel would have run off with the prodigious speed of a snake. The tarantula never retreats. I carefully released it from its glass bell: it landed directly on the anthill. The ants immediately set upon it. The tarantula jumped about the earth and fought desperately, and before long most of the half-eaten ants lay writhing on the ground, dying. Furiously the tarantula attacked anything that moved, choosing not to avail itself of the opportunity to leave, and stood there, as though in wait of new adversaries. The battle lasted over an hour, but finally even the tarantula was drawn into the anthill. I watched the clash with agonizing excitement, and vague memories, forgotten infinitely long ago, glimmered amid the haze of my forever-buried experiences. Immediately after this I set off again: to catch lizards and to pour water into gopher burrows. After a long wait, a little wet beast emerged from the water; it darted off and disappeared down another hole. But neither gophers nor lizards, neither ants nor even the tarantula, could compare with the bizarre sight that I happened upon early one July morning. I saw migrating rats. They travelled in a lopsided rectangle, dragging their tails along the ground and scuttling on their paws. I perched in a tree and watched how quickly the earth turned black as the rats reached a little ravine, disappearing into it only to reappear, squeaking and hurrying onward; how later they reached the Terek, how the plague of them paused for a moment and then, having swum across the river, vanished into someone's garden. I climbed down from the tree and went to lie down by the edge of the forest.

The hush, the sun, the trees... From time to time I could hear the sound of earth falling into a ravine and the cracking of little twigs: a wild boar running. I would doze off on the grass and waken with a damp back and a golden fire before my eyes. Then, looking back at the red, setting sun, I would head home to the cool rooms of my grandfather's apartment and arrive just in time to see the shepherd in his white felt hat driving the flock from pasture; and Grandfather's butting cows, famous for their foul temper and fine milk, would come lowing though the gates of the cattle yard. I knew that the calves would hurry at once to their mothers, that the dairymaid would push the calves' stubborn heads away from their mothers' udders, that those robust jets of milk would ring as they hit the bottom of the white pails, and that Grandfather would look down from the gallery overlooking the yard and tap his cane on the floor, after which he would lose himself in thought, as though recalling some memory. And truly he had much to recall. There had been a time, long ago, when he would steal teams of horses from hostile tribes and sell them. In those days, it was considered a daring feat; and exploits such as these were the subject of unanimous praise. All this took place in the Thirties and Forties of the last century. I remembered Grandfather as a little old man in a Circassian coat with a gold dagger. In 1912 he turned one hundred, but he was hale and sprightly, and old age had mellowed him. He died in the second year of the war, in the saddle of the three-year-old English horse that belonged to his son, my father's eldest brother, which had yet to be broken in. But the incomparable art of riding, for which he had long been famous, betrayed him: he fell from the horse, struck the sharp edge of a kettle that was lying on the ground, and died several hours later. He knew and understood so much, although he was not given to talking; only from the words of other old men, his younger acquaintances, did I gain the impression that Grandfather had been as cunning and clever as a snake—as those ingenuous children of the mid nineteenth century used to say. Grandfather's cunning consisted in the fact that after the Russians' arrival in the Caucasus he left the teams of horses in peace for evermore and took up the quiet life—something that one would never have expected of this spirited man. Each of his friends fell victim to revenge; his house was attacked twice, but on the first occasion he learnt of this in good time and fled with his family; the second time, using his rifle, he mounted a defence for several hours, killed six men, and held out until help arrived. However, the attackers did manage to cause some injury: they felled Grandfather's best apple tree. Grandfather was so proud of his orchard and wouldn't let anyone go there except me. In this orchard grew white transparents, enormous golden plums and oval pears of a terrific size, while through the middle of it, in the depths of a ravine, which in the regional dialect they called a chine, flowed a stream teeming with trout. I would gorge myself on unripe fruits and go around pale-faced and with suffering in my eyes. Aunty would tell Grandfather reproachfully:

"That's what you get for letting the boy into the orchard!"

In point of fact, it was she who governed everything, and, as Grandfather grew older, she gradually took power into her own hands. Ordinarily, though, she never dared contradict Grandfather, and so when she said: that's what you get for letting the boy into the orchard—Grandfather flew into a rage and cried out in his high-pitched, senile voice:

"Shut up!"

She was frightened half to death, went to her room, and lay for a whole hour on the divan, her face buried in the pillow. "Why are you so afraid?" I asked.

"You don't know anything," replied Aunty. "Grandfather will kill me. Your grandfather's a terrible man."

"You're just a coward," I said. "Grandfather's a nice man. He wouldn't lay a finger on you, even though you're mean and wicked. Anyway, why shouldn't I go into the orchard?" I continued, forgetting Grandfather and suddenly losing my temper. "You want all the apples for yourself, don't you? You won't eat them all anyway."

"I'm going to write to your mother and tell her that you've been giving me cheek." But Aunty's threat didn't frighten me in the least, especially since I rarely quarrelled with her: I was much too busy shooting sparrows, hunting cats and roaming the forest. Having spent a month or two at Grandfather's, I would travel on to my beloved Kislovodsk—the only provincial town that resembled a capital in both its customs and appearance. I loved its summer villas that towered up over the streets, its tiny park, its green arcade of grapevines stretching from the railway terminus into town, the crunch of footsteps along the gravel of the Kursaal, and the carefree society that gathered there from every corner of Russia. But from the first years of the war, Kislovodsk became inundated with ruined ladies, washed-up actors, and youths from Moscow and Petersburg; these young folk would go riding on hired horses and waggle their elbows about so frantically, as if someone were shaking them by the arm. At Kislovodsk I would drink cordial diluted with Narzan, go for strolls in the park and hike in the mountains, where high above the town stood a little white building with a portico; it was called the Temple of Air. I never did find out who gave it that pretentious name worthy of some backwater bard with flowing tresses and three years of a local secondary education to his name. But I loved going up there: the wind, like a river of air, babbled and streamed between the columns. The white walls were covered with graffiti, wherein desperate Russian love and the vain yearning to immortalize one's name attained perfection. I loved the red rocks on the mountain, loved even the Castle of Perfidy and Love, where there was a restaurant that served excellent trout. I loved the red sand of the alleyways in Kislovodsk and the white beauties of the Kursaal—northern women with the crimsoned whites of rabbit's eyes. In the park I would pass by the little cliff on the Olkhovka, where a photographer always kept vigil, capturing the women and young ladies who would stand above a falling wall of water; I saw these photographs everywhere I went, even in the furthest reaches of Russia.

"And here is a picture of me in Kislovodsk…"

"Why, yes, of course," I would say. "I know it."

The Kislovodsk of my childhood is engraved in my memory as a white building with sentimental graffiti. But already the evenings were beginning to grow cooler; in early autumn I returned home, once again to sink into that cold and tranquil life that in my imagination is inextricably linked with the crunch of snow, quiet rooms, soft rugs and the plush divans that stood in the parlour. It was as if at home I migrated to some foreign country, where one had to live differently from everywhere else. In the evenings I liked to sit in my room with the light out; the rose-coloured nocturnal blaze of the street lamps would cast its gentle reflection onto my window. The armchair was soft and comfortable, and from the doctor's apartment below would come the slow, hesitant playing of a piano. I would imagine that I was sailing upon a sea and that the spume of white-capped waves was being whipped up before my eyes. When I came to recall this period in my life, it struck me that I had never had an adolescence. I had always sought the company of my elders and at the age of twelve had tried in every conceivable way, despite my obvious appearance, to seem grown-up. At thirteen I studied Hume's *A Treatise on Human Nature* and of my own accord I waded through the history of philosophy that stood on our bookshelf. This reading invested me forever with the habit of adopting a critical stance in relation to everything; it served as an ancillary for my sluggishness of perception and unresponsiveness to external events. My emotions were unable to keep pace with my reason. A sudden love of change that came upon me in fits lured me away from home; there was a time when I began to leave early and return late, spending my time in the company of dubious characters—partners at the billiard table, for which I acquired a taste at thirteen and a half

years of age, a matter of weeks before the revolution.
I remember the thick blue smoke that hung over the
baize, and the players' faces, which would emerge from
the shadows in sharp relief; among them were people
without profession, clerks, brokers and profiteers. I found
several kindred spirits there; and after we had all won, we
would set out at ten o'clock in the evening for the circus,
to watch the women riders; or else to some nightclub,
where lewd ditties were sung and cabaret singers danced;
they would dance, standing on the stage and clasping
their hands below the waist, so that the tips of their left
thumb and index fingers touched the corresponding pair
on the right. This yearning for change and this urge to
leave home coincided with a period heralding a new era
in my life. For a long time it had been on the brink of
arrival; a vague awareness of its mounting inevitability
had always resided within me, but it had been crushed
under the weight of trivia. It was as if I were standing
on the bank of a river, ready to throw myself into the
water, but could not bring myself to do so, all the while
knowing that there was no escaping it; a little more time
would pass, and I would plunge into the water and start
to swim, swept along by its powerful, steady current. It
was the end of spring in 1917: the revolution had come
several months previously, and that summer, in the month

of June, an event to which my life had slowly been leading me finally happened, something for which everything that I had lived and understood until then was but a trial and preparation. One sultry evening following an unbearably hot day, on the playing field of the "Eagle" gymnastics club, as I stood in a leotard and plimsolls, bared to the waist and exhausted, I caught sight of Claire sitting in the stands.

The next morning I returned to the playing field to sunbathe; I lay down on the sand, placed my arms behind my head, and looked up at the sky. The wind ruffled the pleats of my bathing suit, which was a little too large for me. The place was deserted, except that in the shade of the orchard abutting the neighbouring building, Grisha Vorobyov, a student and gymnast, was reading a Mark Krinitsky novel.

"Have you read Krinitsky?"

"No, I haven't."

"Just as well." And with that, Grisha once again fell silent. I closed my eyes and saw an orange haze cut across by bolts of green light. I must have fallen asleep for several minutes, because I heard nothing. Suddenly I felt a cold, gentle hand touching my shoulder. A pure, feminine voice said above me:

"Please don't sleep, comrade gymnast."

I opened my eyes and saw Claire, whose name was still a mystery to me then. "I'm not sleeping," I replied.

"Do you know who I am?" continued Claire.

"No, I saw you for the first time yesterday evening. What's your name?"

"Claire."

"Ah, you're French," I said, cheering up for no apparent reason. "Won't you sit down? Only, it's a little sandy here."

"So I see," said Claire. "I see you're training hard with your gymnastics and can even walk with your hands on the parallel bars. That's quite a sight."

"I learnt to do it at the military academy."

She was silent for a moment. Her nails were long and pink, her hands like alabaster, her body shapely and firm, and her legs long with slender calves. "I believe you have a tennis court here?" Her voice carried the enigma of instantaneous charm, for it always seemed familiar; I even wondered whether I had already heard it somewhere, having managed to forget it and only now remembering it again.

"I'd like to play tennis," the voice announced, "and to sign up for the gymnastics club. Won't you entertain me? You're terribly unobliging."

"How might I entertain you?"

"Show me some gymnastics."

I grasped the hot horizontal bar with my hands and showed her everything I could do, then I made a somersault in the air before sitting down again on the sand. Claire watched me, shading her eyes with her hand; the sun was shining fiercely. "Bravo! Only one day you'll crack your skull open. I don't suppose you play tennis?"

"No."

"How monosyllabic you are. It's obvious you aren't used to talking to women."

"To women?" I said in astonishment. Never had it crossed my mind that there was a particular way of speaking to women. One had to be more polite with them, naturally, but nothing more. "But you aren't even a woman, you're a girl."

"And you know the difference between a woman and a girl, do you?" asked Claire with a laugh.

"I do."

"And who explained it to you? Your aunt?"

"No, I know it myself."

"From experience?" said Claire, again bursting into laughter.

"No," I said, blushing.

"My God, he's blushing!" cried Claire, clapping her hands. All the commotion roused Grisha, who had peacefully fallen asleep over his Mark Krinitsky. He cleared his throat and stood up; his face was marked by a green blade of grass cutting across his cheek.

"Who is this fine-looking and comparatively young man?"

"At your service," said Grisha in a deep voice, still croaky and carrying the echo of sleep. "Grisha Vorobyov."

"You say it with such pride, as if you had just said: Leo Tolstoy."

"A friend of our amiable little club's president," Grisha explained, "and a third-year student in the faculty of law."

"You forgot to add: and a reader of Mark Krinitsky," I ventured.

"Pay no attention to him," said Grisha, turning to Claire. "This youth is awfully immature."

At the time, I was about to move up from year five to year six; Claire was finishing at the gymnasium. She wasn't a resident of our town; her father, a merchant, was in the Ukraine only temporarily. They all—that is, the father and mother, Claire and her elder sister—occupied a whole floor of a large hotel and lived separately from one another. Claire's mother was never at home; her sister, a student at the conservatoire, played the piano and went for strolls in town with the student Yurochka forever trailing behind her, carrying a folder containing her sheet music. Her entire life consisted in these two activities alone—walking and playing; sitting at the piano, she would say quickly, without interrupting her practice: "My God, to think that I still haven't left the house today!"—and while out for a walk she would suddenly remember that she hadn't prepared some exercise or other, and Yurochka, always by her side, would simply clear his throat and transfer the music folder from one hand to the other. Theirs was a strange family. The head of the household, a grey man, always immaculately turned out, seemed to ignore the existence of the hotel in which they lived. He travelled to and from the city in his yellow motor car, spent every evening at the theatre, or in a restaurant, or in a nightclub, and many of his acquaintances did not even suspect that he was raising two daughters and providing for a wife, their mother. Occasionally he would bump into her at the theatre and bow very courteously, while she would respond with that same degree of courteousness, which, incidentally, seemed more pointed and even somewhat mocking.

"Who was that?" the head of the household's companion would ask.

"Who was that?" the man accompanying his wife would ask.

"That was my wife."

"That was my husband."

And they would both smile, and both would know and see: he his wife's smile, and she her husband's. Their daughters were left to their own devices. The elder intended to marry Yurochka; the younger, Claire, maintained a studied indifference towards everyone. At home there were no rules, no appointed hours for eating. I visited their apartment several times. I would arrive straight from the playing field, tired and happy to be with Claire. I loved her room with its white furniture, its large writing desk covered with green blotting paper (Claire never wrote anything), and its leather armchair with lions' heads adorning the armrests. On the floor lay a great blue rug with a design of a prodigiously long horse and a gaunt rider who looked like a jaundiced Don Quixote; the low divan with cushions was soft and sloped towards the window. I even loved the watercolour "Leda and the Swan" that hung on the wall, although the swan was dark-coloured—"It must be a cross between an ordinary swan and an Australian one," I told Claire—and Leda was unpardonably disproportionate. I very much liked the portraits of Claire: she had a great many of them, for she loved herself dearly—and not only the essential, personal things that all people love in themselves, but also her body, her voice, her hands and eyes. Claire was gay and scathing, and may well have known too much for her eighteen years. She would joke with me, make me read humorous stories aloud, dress in men's suits, give herself a little moustache using burnt cork, talk in a deep voice and demonstrate how a "polite young man" ought to behave. Yet despite Claire's japes and the frivolity she invariably brought to our encounters, I didn't always feel at ease in her presence. Claire was at that age when all of a girl's faculties, all the efforts of her coquettishness, her every movement and every thought are the unconscious manifestations of her need for the physical sensation of love, one that is often almost impersonal and turns from the entanglements of mutual relations into something else, something that eludes our understanding and takes on a life of its own, like a plant hidden in a room, filling the air with a tormenting, lingering, irresistible fragrance. I didn't understand any of this at the time, but I was constantly aware of it. I would feel unwell: my voice would crack, I would answer distractedly, grow ashen and, peering at myself in the mirror, wouldn't even recognize my own face. I always imagined that I was sinking into a sweet and fiery liquid as I watched Claire's body beside me and her bright eyes with their long lashes. It was as if Claire understood my predicament: she would sigh and stretch out her whole body—ordinarily she would have sat on the divan—and suddenly she would turn over onto her back, her face altered and teeth clenched. This might have gone on for quite some time had I not stopped visiting Claire soon afterwards, after her mother insulted me. It happened very unexpectedly: I was sitting in Claire's room, as I always did, in the armchair; Claire was lying on the divan; all of a sudden behind the door I heard a woman's deep voice scalding the maid. "My mother," said Claire. "Strange, she's rarely at home at this hour." That very moment, Claire's mother burst into the room without knocking. She was a slight lady of around thirty-four; about her neck she wore a diamond choker, and her hands were decked with enormous emeralds. I was dazzled by this lurid profusion of jewels. She might have been beautiful, but her face was spoilt by thick lips and bright, cruel eyes. I rose and bowed to her. Claire immediately introduced me. Her mother, having scarcely even glanced at me, said: infinitely delighted to meet you—and that very second turned to Claire, with the words:

"*Je ne sais pas pourquoi tu invites toujours des jeunes gens, comme celui-là, qui a sa sale chemise déboutonnée et qui ne sait même pas se tenir.*"[17]

Claire blanched.

"*Ce jeune home comprend bien le français,*"[18] she said.

Her mother looked at me reproachfully, as though I were guilty of something, quickly left the room, slamming the door behind her, and in the corridor shouted:

"Oh, laissez-moi tranquille tous!"[19]

After this episode, I stopped visiting Claire. Late autumn was on the horizon and the tennis season was over; now there was no chance of seeing Claire on the playing field. In response to my letters, she arranged two assignations, but kept neither of them. For four months I didn't see her. By which time it was already winter, and in the woods outside the city, where I would go skiing, the trees jingled like silver from the frost, and daredevils careered down the compacted road to the country restaurant, the Versailles. Ravens flew slowly over the snowy plains that began just beyond the forest. I followed their leisurely flight and would think of Claire; the strange hope of meeting her there suddenly began to seem possible, although there could be no doubt that Claire would never frequent a place like that. But since I was preparing myself for that meeting with her and forgetting all else, my capacity to think rationally was stifled; I was like a man who, having lost his money, searches for it everywhere and, chiefly, where it could never be. All these four months I thought only of Claire. Still I saw before me her diminutive figure, her eyes, her legs in their black stockings. I imagined the conversation that would ensue between us; I heard Claire's laughter and saw her in my dreams. And, slowly gliding on my skis, I would unconsciously search the snow for traces of her. Stopping in the forest to light a cigarette, I would hear the crunch of branches giving way under the weight of the snow, and I would wait for the sound of footsteps at any moment, for a dusting of snow to fly up into the air, and amid this white cloud to see Claire. And although I knew her appearance well, I wouldn't always picture her in the same way; she changed, took on the forms of various women, and came to resemble now Lady Hamilton, now the fairy Rautendelein. I didn't understand my condition then; now, however, I think that all these oddities and changes were like a searchlight suddenly flashing up and down a broad, still strip of water, catching its ripples and its shimmer, while others looking on would have seen in this shimmering the broken image of a sail, the light of a distant home, the white ribbon of a limestone highway, the glittering tail of a fish, and the flickering image of some enormous glass building in which they had never lived. I began to feel cold; I set off once more for the path leading to the city; it was already evening; the snow, rose-hued in the light of the setting sun, spread out all around, and from just beyond the far-off bend in the highway came the jingling of little bells beneath a shaft harness, and their sounds, whispering indistinct melodies, clashed and interrupted one another. Darkness set in; it was as if the air were turning to sapphire—a gem in which an image of the city to which I was returning emerged, the city in which, in the tall white building of a hotel, Claire lived; she's probably, I thought to myself, lying on the divan right now, and that jaundiced Don Quixote will still be galloping silently on the rug, while the dark-grey swan embraces fat Leda; and so the path to Claire stretched out across the earth, directly linking the forest through which I was walking with that room, that divan and Claire encompassed by romantic themes. I waited—and was deceived. Amid these continual mistakes Claire's black stockings, her laughter and her eyes combined to form an inhuman and bizarre image in which the fantastic was mixed with the real, and memories of my childhood with vague forebodings of catastrophe. It was so improbable that many times I wished that I were dreaming and could have woken up. And this state, in which I both was and was not, suddenly began to take on a familiar form; I recognized the pale spectres of my erstwhile wanderings through the unknown—and once again I succumbed to my former illness; every object seemed deceptive and vague, and again the orange flame of a subterranean sun lit up the valley into which I was tumbling in a cloud of yellow sand, onto the bank of a black lake, into my deathly silence. I do not know how much time passed before I saw myself in my bed, in a room with high ceilings. I measured time then by distance and felt as though I had been walking endlessly—until someone's guiding hand stopped me in my tracks. Once, on a hunt, I had seen a wounded wolf trying to escape a pack of dogs. Bounding heavily through the snow, he left a trail of red across the white field. Stopping often, he always forced himself to start running again, and when he fell, it seemed to me as if a terrible earthly force were striving to chain him to the spot and hold him there, a shuddering grey mass, until the dogs' snarling faces could draw near. I believed that this same force, like an enormous magnet, was stopping me in my spiritual wanderings and nailing me to my bed; even now I can hear Nanny's frail voice, reaching me as if from the opposite bank of an invisible blue river:

Oh, I don't see my beloved
In the village, or in town,
Oh, I only ever see him
In the night and in my dreams.

On the wall there hangs a long-familiar drawing by Sipovsky: the rooster that he sketched in the nursery. "Whereas Claire has a swan and Don Quixote," I think, sitting up in bed. "Yes," I tell myself, as if waking and seeing clearly. "Yes, it's Claire. But what is 'it'?" I anxiously think again, and I see that "it" is everything: Nanny, the rooster, the swan, Don Quixote, myself, the blue river that flows through the room—they're all things surrounding Claire. There she lies on the divan, face pale, teeth clenched, breasts protruding under her white blouse; her legs in their black stockings float through the air as though swimming through water, and the fine veins below her knees swell with the blood coursing through them. Beneath her, brown velvet; above her, a stuccoed ceiling; around her, Don Quixote, Leda, the swan and I languish in the forms that have been granted us by fate forever; around us the buildings tower high, encircling Claire's hotel; around us the city, beyond it fields and forests, beyond those fields and forests—Russia; beyond Russia, high up in the sky, motionless, hangs a capsized ocean, the wintry, arctic waters of space. While down below, in the doctor's apartment, someone is playing the piano, and the sounds sway like a pendulum. "Claire, I'm waiting for you," I said aloud. "Claire, I'll always wait for you." And again I saw Claire's pale, disembodied face, and her calves, as though someone had chopped them off and were now showing them to me. "You wanted to see Claire's face, you wanted to see her legs? Well, look." And I looked upon this face as I would have a talking head in a travelling fair, surrounded by wax figures in bizarre costume, beggars, tramps and murderers. But why, I thought, were all these fragments of myself and everything among which I led so many different lives—this crowd of people and this never-ending clamour of sounds and all the rest: snow, trees, buildings, the valley with the black lake—why was all this suddenly embodied within me, and I cast down onto this bed, condemned to lie for hours before an ethereal portrait of Claire, to be this idle companion of hers, just like Don Quixote and Leda, to become a romantic figure, and after so many years to lose myself again, as in childhood, as before, as always? Even after my illness had passed, I went on living as though I were in a deep black well, above which, continually materializing and changing, reflected in the water's murky mirror, Claire's pale face appeared. The well swayed, like a tree in the wind, and Claire's reflection kept lengthening and widening before, with a shiver, it disappeared.

More than anything else, I adored snow and music. When there was a blizzard and it seemed as if nothing else in the world existed—no houses, no earth, but only a white smoke, the wind and the whispering air—I would sometimes think, as I made my way through this living expanse, that if the legend of the world's creation had been born in the north, then the first words in the Good

Book would have been: "In the beginning was the blizzard." When it had subsided, from under the snow a whole world would suddenly appear, like a forest in a fairy tale growing out of someone's cosmic desire; I would see those twisting rows of black buildings and snowdrifts gathering with a rush of air, and little figures walking about the streets. I especially enjoyed watching birds flying through the snow and swooping down to the ground during the blizzard: they would fold and unfurl their wings, as if not wanting to be parted from the wind—but still they would land, and immediately, as if by magic, they would be transformed into black lumps walking around on invisible legs, and they would flutter their wings with a particular birdlike movement, which for some reason was singularly comprehensible to me. I had long since stopped believing in God and angels, but since childhood I had preserved a mental image of the heavenly host; I didn't believe that these beautiful winged people would fly or sit like birds, that they would make those quick movements, for such beating of wings betrays restlessness. Whenever I watched birds descending from a great height, I was always reminded of a slain eagle. I would remember how Father once came back from an unsuccessful boar hunt, his rifle slung over his shoulder. I went running up to him. I would have been around eight at the time. He took me by the hand, then looked up and said:

"Look, Kolya. Do you see that bird flying?"

"Yes."

"That's an eagle."

Very high up in the air, with its wings outstretched, there really was an eagle soaring; now tilting to one side, now levelling out again, it seemed to pass over us slowly. It was very hot and bright. "An eagle can look at the sun without blinking," I mused. At length Father took aim, tracking the eagle's flight in the sight of his rifle. Then he fired. The eagle immediately jerked up as if the bullet had tossed it up in the air, and it flapped its wings several times in quick succession before falling. It spun around on the ground like a top and opened its filthy beak: its feathers were bloody. "Stay back!" Father shouted, just as I was about to go racing over to the spot where the bird had fallen. I approached the eagle only after it had stopped moving. It lay there on the earth, its broken wing crooked and half-open, its head with its bloodied beak tucked under, and its yellow eye already glazing over. Around one of its legs gleamed a copper band with something scrawled on it. "It's an old one," Father muttered. I always remembered this whenever there was a blizzard, because it was during a blizzard that I recalled the slain eagle for the first time; I was in a park, on skis, and the blizzard had forced me to take shelter in a little cabin that stood in the middle of a forest on the outskirts of the city. Inside this cabin was a ski station. After waiting for the blizzard to pass, I ventured out again into the forest: my skis sank deeply into the soft, newly fallen snow. After a while, a frost set in and the whole sky momentarily turned red. "There'll be a wind," I thought. But for now it was quiet. "There'll be a wind," I repeated aloud. And just then, far, far off in the forest, I suddenly heard a tinkling. Whether it was the icicles falling from the trees or a light wind catching one of those stalactites hanging in the firs, I don't know. I know only that after it had passed silence fell again—and then once more the ice began to tinkle. It was as if a little forest dwarf living in a cave were quietly playing a glass violin. And suddenly the enormous terrestrial expanse seemed to roll up like a geographical map, and instead of Russia I now found myself in the fabled Black Forest. Behind the trees, woodpeckers were tapping away; white snowy mountains dreamt above the lakes' icy plains; and down below, in the valley, a delicate net, hardening in the frosty air, floated with a jingle. In that moment, as whenever I was truly happy, I vanished from my own consciousness. It could happen in a forest, in a field, on a river, by the seashore; it could happen while I was reading a captivating book. Even then, I was overwhelmed by the imperfection and transience of that silent concert surrounding me wherever I went. It would pass through me, and along the way marvellous landscapes, unforgettable smells, cities in Spain, dragons and beauties rose up and faded away—while I remained a strange being whose arms and legs were of no use, who bore upon his back a whole host of unwieldy and useless things. My life seemed not to be my own. I dearly loved my home, my family, but in my dreams I often saw myself roaming our city, passing by the building in which I lived—forever passing it by, unable to enter, for I had to keep going. Something was always compelling me to strive onward, as though there might have been something new to see. I often had this dream. I carried within myself an infinite number of familiar thoughts, feelings and images—and I felt nothing of their burden. But whenever I thought of Claire, my body would fill up with molten metal, and everything that preoccupied me—ideas, memories, books—all this would invariably rush to cast off its usual guise, and Brehm's *Life of Animals* or the dying eagle would inevitably metamorphose into Claire's slender calves, her blouse through which I espied the round tormenting shadows about her nipples, her eyes and her face. I tried not to think of Claire, but only on rare occasions did I succeed. Then again, there were evenings when I didn't think about her at all: or, rather, the thought of her lay submerged in the depths of my consciousness, while it seemed to me as if I were forgetting her.

One evening, very late at night, I was walking home from the circus—without a thought for Claire. It was snowing heavily; the cigar that I was smoking kept going out. The streets were deserted and all the windows were dark. I recalled as I went a little ditty that the clown had sung:

> *I'm not a Bolshevik,*
> *I'm not a Menshevik,*
> *Ah, I'm a people's commissar…*

and a curious, unsteady resonance still reverberated in my ear, as when a singer plays a musical instrument and croons along to its melodic accompaniment. I had, moreover, the sudden feeling that something was about to happen—and then, thinking about it, I realized that I had long since been aware of footsteps following me. I turned around. Enswathed in the fox collar of her fur coat, as though in a cloud of gold, her eyes wide open and gazing at me through the slowly falling snow, Claire was walking behind me. Suddenly, from around the corner, I thought I heard the rapid patter of running water on the pavement, then the striking of a hammer against stone—and immediately afterwards came the silence that I heard during my bouts of illness. My breathing grew laboured; a haze of snow stood all around me—and everything that happened next did so despite me and apart from me. I found it difficult to speak, and Claire's voice reached me as though from afar. "Hello, Claire," I said, "I haven't seen you in a long time."

"I've been busy," replied Claire with a laugh. "I've married."

Claire's married now, I thought without comprehension. Yet the terrible custom that obliges one to continue a conversation somehow clung to a small portion of my slipping attention, and I answered, and spoke, and even grieved all the while. But everything that I uttered was false and didn't correspond to my emotions. Still laughing and staring at me—and now I recall how for a split second her pupils flashed with fright when she realized that she wouldn't be able to draw me out of this state of sudden torpidity—Claire told me that she had been married for nine months, but that she had no desire to ruin her figure. "That's nice," I muttered, understanding only the line about her not wanting to spoil her figure; but as to why her figure might be spoilt, I neither heard nor understood. At any other time, this simple declaration of not wanting to spoil her figure would of course have surprised me, just as it would were someone to have told me, apropos of nothing: I don't want to cut off my leg.

"You'll have to reconcile yourself to the fact that I'm no longer a girl: I've become a woman. Do you remember our first conversation?"

"Reconcile myself?" I thought, latching on to these words. "Yes, I'll have to reconcile myself… I'm not angry with you, Claire," I said.

"It doesn't scare you?" Claire went on.

"No, on the contrary."

We were walking together now; I had given Claire my arm. All around us snow was falling in great flakes.

"Take this down in French." I heard Claire's voice, and it took me a second to remember who was talking to me. "*Claire n'est plus vierge.*"[20]

"Very well," I said. "*Claire n'est plus vierge.*"

When we reached her hotel, she said: "My husband is out of town. My sister is spending the night at Yurochka's. Mama and Papa are also away."

"You'll sleep peacefully, then, Claire."

But once again Claire began to laugh.

"I should hope not."

She suddenly came up to me and with both hands took me by the collar of my greatcoat.

"Let's go to my room," she said sharply. Through the fog in front of me, at a significant distance, I saw her motionless face. I stood rooted to the spot. Her face again drew closer, and it grew wrathful.

"Have you gone mad or are you unwell?"

"No, no," I said.

"Whatever is the matter with you?"

"I don't know, Claire."

She went up without saying goodbye; I heard her close the door and stand for a minute at the threshold. I wanted to go after her but I couldn't. Snow was still falling and disappearing into thin air, and everything that I had known and loved until then eddied and vanished with it. I didn't sleep for two nights after that. Some while later I ran into Claire in the street again; I bowed to her, but she didn't acknowledge me.

In the ten years separating these two encounters with Claire, nowhere and at no point did I ever forget this. At times I would regret that I hadn't died there and then; at others I would imagine myself to be Claire's beloved. Even as a vagabond sleeping under the open skies of barbarous Asiatic lands, I still remembered the look of wrath on her face, and after the passage of many years I would wake up in the middle of the night with a feeling of infinite regret, whose origin I would fail to grasp at once—and only later would I divine that its source was my memory of Claire. Once again I would see her—through the snow and the blizzard and the silent tumult of the greatest shock of my life.

———

I cannot recall a time when—regardless of circumstance or company—I wasn't certain that one day in the distant future I should find myself living in a different place, in a different manner. I was always ready for change, even when there was no change to be envisaged, and I lamented, long before the fact, losing that circle of friends and acquaintances to which I had managed to accustom myself. I sometimes imagined that this continual sense of anticipation was independent of both external circumstances and my love of change; rather, that it was something innate and immutable, and possibly just as vital as vision or hearing. And yet, there had of course always been some elusive connection between the strain of this anticipation and other influences that bore upon me, but it was impervious to any rational explanation. I remember sitting in a park not long before my departure (which matter, at that point, had yet to be settled), and suddenly I heard Polish being spoken beside me; amid the flow of speech the words *wszystko* and *bardzo* rang out over and again. I felt a chill run down my spine and I was overcome by a powerful resolve: now I simply had to go. What bearing could these words have had on the course of events in my life? But, hearing them, I knew that there could no longer be any doubt. I don't know whether such conviction would have materialized had I heard, instead of the Polish being spoken beside me, the call of a thrush or the cuckoo's melancholy song. I turned to observe carefully this person saying *wszystko* and *bardzo*; he was evidently a Polish Jew, whose face betrayed a look of fright, a readiness to smile at the least provocation, and perhaps even a barely notice-able, barely discernible, but nevertheless unmistakable baseness. Such are the faces of parasites and gigolos. Sitting beside him was a girl of twenty-two or so; she wore rings on her reddened fingers with their long dirty nails, had mournful, jaded eyes and a particular sort of smile that would suddenly endear her to any man who happened to look her way. Never again did I set eyes on these people, although I remembered them very well, as if I had known them for a long, long time. Then again, strangers always did interest me. Their distinction came in contrast to acquaintances, who became homely, safe and, in consequence, uninteresting. Back then it seemed to me that every stranger knew something that I couldn't divine; I could distinguish between simple unknowns and strangers *par excellence*, a type that existed in my imagination like that of the foreigner—which is to say, a person not only of different nationality, but who belonged to a different world, one that was inaccessible to me. Perhaps my feelings for Claire were in part because she was French and a foreigner. Although she spoke Russian with perfect fluency and accuracy and understood everything down to the meaning of folk sayings, there remained in her a certain charm that a Russian girl would never have. And her French, to my ear, was imbued with a strange, miraculous delight, notwithstanding the fact that French came easily to me and that, by all accounts, I too should have known its musical secrets. Not as well as Claire, of course, but I ought to have known all the same. Then again, I always unconsciously coveted the unknown, wherein I hoped to discover new opportunities and new lands. I believed that contact with the unknown would cause everything that was important to me, all my knowledge, strength, desire to understand something new, suddenly to rise up and manifest itself in a purer form: having understood everything, I would thereby subordinate it to myself. It was this same covetousness, only in an altered form, that I then believed to have moved knights and lovers:

the knights' crusades and the lovers' genuflection before foreign princesses—all this was an unquenchable thirst for knowledge and power. But here a contradiction arose, in that there were direct causes of the knights' crusades, causes in which they themselves believed and for which they had gone to war. And were these causes not real, while the others were fictitious? History, Romanticism, art—they all came into being only after the event serving as their stimulus had died and no longer existed, while what we read and think of them is but the play of shadows inhabiting our imagination. And just as in childhood I had devised my own adventures on board the pirate ship about which Father told me, so later I created kings, conquistadors and beauties, forgetting that sometimes beauties proved to be coquettes, conquistadors murderers and kings' fools; and the red-bearded giant Barbarossa never spared a thought for knowledge, or fantasy, or love for the unknown; and perhaps, as he drowned in the river, he didn't recall what he might have done, had he submitted to the laws of that imaginary life of his, which we created for him many centuries after his death. When I thought about all this, everything seemed so unreal and vague, like a shadow passing through smoke. And once again I would turn from such strained but arbitrary perceptions to what I saw around me, and to a more intimate knowledge of the people surrounding me; this was all the more important, for I sensed the already-approaching necessity of forsaking them and, perhaps, never seeing them again. But when I fixed my attention on them, I saw more often their shortcomings and foibles than their merits; this derived in part from my incapacity to be a good judge of character, and in part from the fact that my critical attitude towards them was strong, while the art of appreciating and understanding them was almost totally lacking in me. That particular art manifested itself only much later, and even then it would not infrequently prove wrong, though at times it was very sincere and pure-intentioned. I took pleasure in loving certain people without growing overly attached to them, for there was always a part of them that would remain unexpressed, and though I knew full well that whatever went unsaid was bound to be plain and ordinary, still I unwittingly constructed for myself illusions that would not have existed were it not for this inexpressibility. Of all such people, Boris Belov was the one I loved most. An engineer who had just finished at the technical institute, he was known for his perpetual frivolity, and when the cadet Volodya, who had a marvellous singing voice (he was on leave from some detachment of partisans, and whenever introducing him to someone Belov would say: "Vladimir, partisan and crooner") sang the romance "Stillness" in the Voronins' parlour and reached the part when the moon swims out from behind the lindens, behind his back Belov mimed a floating moon, waving his arms and puffing out his cheeks, like a man who has fallen into water. Just as Volodya stopped singing, Belov said:

"I'd give a lot of money for irrefutable proof that the moon really does swim and that lindens are indeed made from lace." And the artist Severny, who found himself in their presence, remarked with a sorrowful smile:

"How you do joke…" For he himself never joked, since he was incapable of it, and therefore had little liking for jokers. He was an eternally and immutably sad figure. "He's incorrigible," Belov was wont to say of him, "the very champion of melancholy." Yet the most astonishing thing about him was that no other man on earth could match his incredible appetite. "Come, Severny, why are you always so morose?" some girl would ask him. And Severny, with a bitter smile and looking vacantly into the middle distance, would reply: "It's difficult to say…" And the terrific pause that would follow this phrase would be broken by Belov, declaiming: whom might I tell of my sorrow? For all that, though, Belov proved to be much more than just a joker; once, turning up at Belov's unannounced, I heard someone playing Torelli's violin sonata and saw that it was none other than Belov himself. "What, you play the violin?" I asked, astonished. He simply replied, without a hint of irony, as usual:

"Nothing in the world can compare with music."

Whereupon he added:

"And it grieves me to be so utterly bereft of talent."

Then he suddenly recollected himself and, having repeated that phrase about nothing comparing with music (though this time in his usual tone of voice), added: "Except, perhaps, muskmelon?…" He pretended to think. But I already knew what it was that he thought necessary to hide—he, who poked fun at everyone, was never more afraid than when he opened himself to ridicule. And so afterwards Belov began to act more reservedly around me than he had done before.

The artist Severny was a man of very narrow views. He was usually taciturn, but on the rare occasion that he took it upon himself to speak, he would invariably spout nonsense. He was greatly satisfied with his paintings, his appearance and his success with women. "You know," he would say, "I'm really quite a looker. Just the other day I was coming out of the theatre, when a famous actress comes running up to me all aflutter. 'Who are you?' she asks. 'What's your name? Listen, I'll go and wait for you at home…' What was I to do? I smiled regrettably"—those were his exact words:

I smiled regrettably—"and replied: 'My dear, I don't care for actresses.' She bit her lip until she drew blood, tapped her fan against her chin and, turning sharply, left. I shrugged."

"I must write this down," said Belov. "You say she bit her lip and sharply turned, to say nothing of the blows of the fan on her chin? And you smiled regrettably?" Severny said nothing and began to talk of his studio. His studio was, incidentally, a neat little room with symmetrically arranged paintings. Belov, who once visited it, was struck by a sketch of a bird's head holding some dark morsel in its beak, which distantly recalled a scrap of iron. Below the painting were the words 'Étude of a Swan'. Belov asked mistrustfully: an *étude*?

"An *étude*," Severny replied firmly.

"And just what is an *étude*?"

"Well, you see," replied Severny after a momentary pause, "it's a sort of French word." He cast around and his gaze fell on Smirnov, his closest friend and a devotee of his talent. With a nod of the head, Smirnov approved Severny's words.

Smirnov understood nothing about painting, just as he understood nothing that exceeded the limits of his rather meagre knowledge. He had studied at the same gymnasium as I but was three years ahead of me; by the time of his friendship with Severny, he was a student at the local university. He always carried revolutionary pamphlets, proclamations and a ready supply of ideas on co-operatives and collectivism, yet his knowledge of these issues derived only from popular books, and when it came to the history of socialism, he was weak and knew nothing of Saint-Simon's sectarianism, Owen's bankruptcy or the mad bookkeeper who waited his entire life for some great eccentric to give him a million so that he could use this money to build happiness first in France, and then across the entire globe. I asked Smirnov:

"Haven't you had enough of those pamphlets?"

"Those pamphlets will help us liberate the people." I refrained from arguing with him, but Belov weighed in on the conversation. "Are you quite certain that the people won't manage without you?" he asked. "If everyone were to reason like that, we'd never become a conscious nation," Smirnov replied. "Just look," said Belov, turning to me, "at what pamphlets have done to this pleasant young man. Never has there existed anywhere a 'conscious nation'. Why, all of a sudden, should we become conscious with the help of some semi-literate pamphlets? And will Smirnov read to us about the evolution of axiology, and Martha, our cook, a woman of exceeding virtue, about the early Renaissance? Smirnov, give these pamphlets to Severny. Tell him that they're *études*." But here it turned out that Severny had long since been a communist and a Party member. Delighted to hear this, Belov shook Severny's hand and said:

"Well, congratulations, my dear fellow. And there I was, thinking you only sketched *études*."

Smirnov, who forever spoke in that strange and pompous language of agitprop, remarked:

"Your trivializing irony, Comrade Belov, could alienate valuable workers from our ranks."

"This isn't a man," said Belov with conviction, turning to me and Severny. "No, this is a newspaper. Not even a newspaper but a leading article. You are a leading article, do you understand?"

"I understand perhaps more than you think."

"What verbs!" uttered Belov derisively. "To understand, to think. The co-operative ideology doesn't exactly hold much truck with those." But Belov's mockery had no effect on either Severny or Smirnov, for, their stupidity aside, they were held to ransom by the fashions that dictated the political discussions and socio-economic debates of the day. These fashions left me indifferent; I was interested only in such abstract ideas that I found relevant, ideas that held a valuable and important personal significance. I could sit for hours poring over a book by Böhme, yet I found it impossible to read treatises on the co-operative. And while I found political discussion—about Russia and revolution—strange, I found their sense, or rather their movement, utterly foreign. I thought about them as I did everything else, most often at night: a lamp shining over my desk, the cold and darkness outside, and I, living as though on some far-flung island. And instantly, no sooner than my mind had conjured them into being, spectres would crowd around outside the window and enter my room. The air was cold in Russia then, and the snow was deep; the buildings loomed black, music played and everything flowed by before me—and everything was so unreal, everything would grind to a halt only to start moving again all of a sudden. One image followed on the heels of another, as if the wind were fanning the flame of a candle, and flickering shadows would begin to leap across the wall, summoned there suddenly by Lord knows what power, flying there for Lord knows what reason, like the silent black visions of my dreams. But when my eyes had wearied I would close them, and it was as if a door had been slammed in my face; and from the darkness and the depths was born a subterranean noise, which I heard without seeing, without comprehending its meaning, attempting to grasp it and remember it. I heard in it the crunch of sand and the rumble of the trembling earth, the plunging howl of someone's hurtling flight and the strains of accordions and barrel organs; and ultimately, as clear as a bell, I heard the voice of a lame soldier:

The Moscow fire burned and roared…

And then I opened my eyes again and saw smoke and red flames twilighting the cold winter streets. It was exceptionally cold at the time: at school, for instance—I was now in the sixth year—we sat there without taking off our overcoats, and our teachers went about in fur coats. They were very rarely paid their salaries, but still they always showed up on time for lessons. There were several subjects that had nobody to teach them, and so there were free periods—and we used this freedom to sing, as a whole class, the convict songs we had learnt from Perenko, a tall boy of eighteen or so who lived in the troubled outskirts of town and had grown up among the thieves and, quite possibly, the murderers of tomorrow. He carried a switchblade, always used thieves' cant, and had a particular way of clicking his tongue and spitting though his teeth. He was a wonderful friend but a poor student—not because he lacked aptitude, but rather because his parents were simple folk and there was no one in his family to help him with his studies. In their little flat adjoining the carpenter's workshop that his father owned, no one had heard of the Hundred Years War or the Wars of the Roses, and so all these names, and foreign words, and the thorny problems of modern history, just like the laws of thermodynamics and passages from the classics of French and German literature—all this was so foreign to Perenko that he couldn't understand it, nor could he commit it to memory or, in the final analysis, even sense that it might one day be of any use to him whatsoever. Perenko might have been interested in these things, had his spiritual needs not found another outlet. But, as with the majority of such people, he was given to sentimentality and would sing his convict songs almost with tears in his eyes: for him, those songs replaced the spiritual thrill afforded by books, music and the theatre, the need for which was quite possibly stronger in him than it was in his more cultivated classmates. The majority of teachers failed to realize this and held Perenko simply to be a troublemaker; it was only the Russian master who took him seriously, paid any attention to him and never laughed at his ignorance, for which Perenko loved him dearly and set him apart from the others. This teacher seemed to us a strange man, because during his lessons he didn't talk of the things we were used to, things that I had been taught over and over again in my five years of secondary education, before I moved schools—that is, to the one where Vasily Nikolaevich taught, for his name was Vasily Nikolaevich. "I've just given you the name Leo Tolstoy," he would say. "The people, you know, held him in the highest regard. My mother, for instance, who was an altogether simple woman, a seamstress, took it into her head to go and see Tolstoy after the death of my father, to ask his advice: what was she to do? Her situation was bad and she was a very poor woman. She wanted to see Tolstoy because she believed him to be the last saint and man of wisdom on earth. You and I will have differing opinions, but my mother was simpler than we, and she wouldn't likely have understood the psychologies of Anna Karenina, of Prince Andrei, and least of all that of Hélène, the Princess Bezukhov; her ideas were uncomplicated, although stronger and more sincere for it; and this, gentlemen, is a great happiness." Then he would start on Tredyakovsky, explaining the difference between syllabic and tonic versification, and observe by way of conclusion:

"Tredyakovsky was an unfortunate man who lived in cruel times. His position was one of humiliation; just imagine, what with the vulgarity of court manners back then, his role—something betwixt a jester and a poet. Derzhavin was far more fortunate than he."

In his appearance and manner Vasily Nikolaevich resembled an Old Believer—his grey beard, his simple iron spectacles; he spoke rapidly, in that northern Russian tongue, which in the Ukraine sounds so astonishing. His dress was shabby; on seeing him in the street, anyone who didn't know him would never have suspected that this old man was a brilliant and erudite pedagogue. There was something ascetic about him: I remember his scowling grey brow and his bloodshot eyes that peered out through his spectacles. I remember his sincerity, courage and simplicity: he never hid his convictions, which might have seemed much too left-wing under the hetman and much too right-wing under the Bolsheviks, or the fact that this mother was a seamstress—a fact to which a man of his station would rarely have owned. Under his tutelage we studied Archpriest Avvakum, and Vasily Nikolaevich would read us long excerpts:

After the sun had dawned on the Sabbath day, they placed me in a cart and stretched out mine arms and conveyed me from the Patriarch's court to the Monastery of Andronicus, and there they clapped me in irons and threw me into a dark cell dug of the earth, and there I sat for three days and neither ate nor drank; sitting in the darkness, I bowed down in my chains I know not whether to east or west. None came to me but mice and black beetles, while crickets chirped and there were fleas aplenty. It came to pass that on the third day I hungered, which is to say that I desired to eat, and after vespers there stood before me I know not whether an angel or a man, and to this very day I know not, but only that he spake a prayer in the darkness and, taking me by the shoulder, led me with my chains unto a bench and sat me down there, and gave me a spoon in my hands and a morsel of bread, and some cabbage soup for to sup—oh, but the taste was uncommon good!—and said unto me: "Enough, that will suffice thee for thy strengthening." And then he was no more... I was entrusted to the guard of a monk and the order was given that I be hoven into the church. By the church they pulled at my hair and prodded at my sides and tugged on my chain and spat in mine eyes. May God forgive them in this life and the next, for it is not their doing but that of Satan, the Evil one.

Also:

Likewise another officer, at another time, found occasion to be moved with fury against me—he broke into my house, beat me and buried in my finger, like a dog, his clutch of teeth. And when his throat was gorged with blood, then did he release my finger from his teeth and, leaving me, went his way. Thanking God, I wrapped my hand in cloth and betook myself unto vespers. As I was on my way, the same man set upon me again with two small pistols and, being near me, fired from one of them, and, by the will of God, while the powder did explode in the pan, yet the pistol did not shoot. He cast it upon the ground, and fired now from the other, and the will of God was exercised again—and the second pistol did not shoot. Walking on, I prayed fervently to God and raised one hand to make the sign of the cross over the officer and bowed deeply before him. He cursed me; and I said unto him: "Let His grace be upon thy lips, Ivan Rodionovich!" He grew enraged by my devotion at church; his will was that the office be done with dispatch, whereas I sang it according to the custom, without haste. Thereupon he deprived me of my house and drove me out onto the road, plundering everything and leaving me without a penny for the journey.

He read terribly well. My classmate Shchur, one of the cleverest and most able individuals that I ever happened to meet, would say to me: "You know, Vasily Nikolaevich is just like Archpriest Avvakum; people like that were burnt at the stake."

"Who here does not know the legend of the dancing Virgin Mary?" Vasily Nikolaevich asked one day. Only one boy in the class knew the legend. He was a Jewish boy by the name of Rosenberg, and he had a tender, childlike face; he was so small that, to look at, one would have thought him eleven or twelve, whereas in actual fact he had already turned sixteen. In the mornings, girls from the eighth year, on seeing him in the street, would shout: little boy, little boy, hurry up, you'll be late!—and Rosenberg would be embarrassed to the point of tears. He was much cleverer and more developed than one might expect of his tender years: he read and remembered much, and often he knew strange things that he had once read in some great almanac and had lodged in his memory: the manufacture of fertilizer in Mexico, religious superstitions of the Polynesians and various anecdotes pertaining to the genesis of English parliamentarianism. And so Rosenberg also knew the legend of the dancing Virgin Mary—because, he said after being called upon by Vasily Nikolaevich to explain, who could not know it? Nevertheless, the majority of the pupils had never heard of this legend, and so Vasily Nikolaevich recounted it to us: we all listened attentively, and Perenko, who until then had been admiring his switchblade, remained in his seat, deep in thought, his eyes trained on the white metal. A couple of days later, Vasily Nikolaevich asked us to read the beginning of the latest biography of Tolstoy, which told of the Ant Brothers—and even Rosenberg knew nothing of the Ant Brothers. That same day the new priest, who had just arrived at school wearing a silk cassock and lacquered bootees, took against me. He entered the classroom for the first time, crossed himself (rather coquettishly, I thought) and surveyed the pupils before saying:

"Gentlemen, it seems that nowadays the word of God and the history of the Church are not in fashion." He shook his head, twisted his lips and sniggered ironically. "Perhaps there are atheists among you, who do not wish to participate in my lessons? Well then"—he smiled mockingly and threw up his hands—"let them stand up and leave the class." As he said the words "leave the class", he grew serious and stern, as if to underscore that he had done with mocking the ignorant atheists and that, of course, there could be no question of anyone wanting to leave the class. This man was bathed in hubris and never let slip an occasion to remind us that religion was now persecuted and that at times remarkable courage was demanded of its ministers—as it was at the dawn of Christianity—and he would cite passages from the sacred texts, continually misquoting them, however, and forcing St John to utter what were nearly the words of

Thomas Aquinas. That being said, I don't believe that the distinction was of such great consequence in his eyes: he wasn't defending religious dogma—a weak spot of his—but something else entirely. And this something else found expression in his habit of being "persecuted", and little by little he grew so firmly accustomed to this role that, were religion to have enjoyed a renaissance in popular esteem, there would have been nothing for him to do at all and he would, very likely, have found life very tedious and boring.

I stood up and left the classroom. He followed me with his gaze and said: "Do you recall the part in the liturgy: 'Catechumens, depart!'?"

A week later Vasily Nikolaevich asked me: "You, Sosedov, do you believe in God?"

"No," I replied. "Do you, Vasily Nikolaevich?"

"I'm a very devout man. He who believes with all his heart shall find happiness."

On the whole the words Vasily Nikolaevich used most often were "happy" and "unhappy". He ranked among those irreconcilable Russians who perceive the meaning of life in the search for truth, even if they are convinced that truth, in the sense in which they comprehend it, does not and cannot exist. His instruction in the Russian language was forever associated with observations on all manner of things, often having no direct bearing on the subject at hand, with dissertations on the modern age, religion and history—and throughout it all he exhibited a remarkable erudition. It would suddenly come to light that he had been abroad, had an impressive knowledge of foreign languages, had lived for some considerable time in Switzerland, England and France and was sensitive to all that he had seen there: he was always searching for his truth, wherever he happened to be. Later I often wondered: would he ever find it, did he have the courage to deceive himself—and would he die a peaceful death? And it struck me that even if by some miracle he fancied he had discovered it, he would likely hasten to renounce it—only to search anew. Perhaps his truth lacked the naïve idea that it is possible to obtain what we have never possessed; certainly it didn't consist in a dream of peace and quiet, for the intellectual inertia to which he would have been condemned would have been a source of shame and torment for him. Vasily Nikolaevich was one of the few teachers I liked throughout my time at the various institutions. All the others were narrow, cared only for their careers and regarded teaching merely as employment. Worst of all were the priests, who made the most obtuse and ignorant educators. Only my first religious instructor, a scholar and a philosopher, seemed to me a rather remarkable man, albeit a fanatic. He was not a pedant: in my fifth year, when I questioned him at great length on the atheistic meaning of the "Grand Inquisitor" and Renan's *Life of Jesus*—I was reading Dostoevsky and Renan at the time, instead of studying the curriculum (I never did learn the catechism or the history of the Church)—never did he take me to task, and only in the last term did he finally beckon me over with his finger and quietly say:

"Kolya"—he called everyone by their familiar name, since he had taught us from our first year—"do you think I've no idea just how little of the catechism you know? Dear boy, I know everything. But I'll still give you full marks, since you at least take some interest in religion. Off you go." When he delivered his sermons tears would well in his eyes, but apparently he didn't believe in God. He reminded me of the Grand Inquisitor in miniature: he was unassailable in dialectical matters and in fact would have made a better Catholic. He had, moreover, a marvellous voice—powerful and intelligent—for it has come to my attention time and again that a man's voice, just like his face, may be intelligent or stupid, talented or inept, noble or base. He was killed several years later, during the Civil War, somewhere in the south—and the news of his death was all the more painful to me, since generally I cared nothing for priests and, as a consequence, had treated this man, who no longer ranked among the living, poorly.

I don't really know why I harboured this dislike for those in holy orders; it may well have been the result of some conviction that they were of lower social standing than others—they and the police. One could never shake their hand, never invite them to dinner. I remember the imposing figure of the district policeman who would come every month to collect his pay-off—Lord knows for what. He would wait patiently in the hallway while the maid fetched him the money, after which he would give a sprightly cough and be on his way, clicking the enormous spurs of his lacquered boots with their exceedingly short collars—the sort worn only by district policemen and, for some reason, the cantors of church choirs. Once, in my third year at school, I saw how even clergymen could be bribed. I had taken ill the fortnight before Easter and so had been unable to fast before taking the Eucharist at the school church. Father Ioann told me that, come autumn, I would have to bring a certificate of fasting, otherwise I wouldn't be allowed to progress and would have to repeat the year. As usual, I spent that summer at Kislovodsk. My uncle Vitaly, a sceptic and romantic who had always remained a captain in the Dragoon Guards because he had challenged his regimental commander to a duel and, in response to his refusal to fight, had given him a slap in the face at an officers' meeting—something for which he spent five years imprisoned in a fortress, emerging a much-changed man and having acquired an astonishing erudition, most uncommon in an officer, in matters of art, philosophy and social sciences, before returning to serve in that same regiment, though never moving up the ranks—he told me:

"Kolya, take ten roubles and go and see this long-maned idiot. Ask him for a certificate. There's no point in your going to church and loafing around there. Just give him the money and take the certificate."

Uncle Vitaly was forever giving everyone a dressing-down and was never satisfied with anyone, although in his private dealings and relations with people he was generally kind and gentle. Whenever Aunty tried to punish her eight-year-old son, he would take him under his protection and say: "Leave him be, he doesn't understand what he's done. Don't you forget, the child is breathtakingly stupid; and if you give him a thrashing, he'll never grow any brains. In any case, it's bad to beat children; it's only unenlightened women like you who don't know that." He began almost every one of his tirades with the words "These idiots…"

"The priest won't give me the certificate that easily," I said. "I'll have to start fasting all over again."

"What utter nonsense. Pay the man ten roubles and be done with it. Do as I tell you."

So I went to the priest. He lived in a little apartment with two canary-yellow armchairs and portraits of bishops on the walls. In response to my request for a certificate, he said:

"My child"—I cringed at this form of address—"come to church, first confess, then receive the sacraments, and afterwards, in a week's time, you shall have your certificate."

"May I not have it now?"

"No."

"But I'd like it now, Father."

"Impossible," said the priest, growing angry at my obstinacy. I then extracted the ten roubles and placed them on the table, but for shame I didn't dare to look at the priest. He took the money and, holding aside the skirt of his cassock and revealing beneath it a pair of narrow black trousers with foot straps, pocketed it before calling out: "Reverend Deacon!" From the neighbouring room the deacon appeared, chewing on something; his face was covered in sweat from the terrific heat and, since he was very fat, it literally streamed off him. Radiant droplets hung from his brows.

"Give this young man a certificate of fasting."

The deacon nodded and immediately wrote out the certificate for me—quite beautifully, in his distinctive block handwriting.

"What did I tell you?" Uncle muttered. "I know their sort, my boy…"

Auntie remarked to him:

"You shouldn't say such things to the boy."

To which he replied:

"This boy, just like any other boy, understands no less than you do. And, Lord, don't I know it! The day you teach me anything will be the day I hang myself."

In the evenings Uncle Vitaly would sit outside on the terrace, immersed in thought. "Why do you spend so long sitting on the terrace?" I would ask. "I immerse myself in thought," Uncle Vitaly would reply, and he imbued this turn of phrase with such a quality, as if he really were immersing himself in thought—as one might in water in a bathtub. Occasionally he would talk with me:

"What year are you in?"

"The fourth."

"What are they teaching you these days?"

"All kinds of subjects."

"They're teaching you a lot of rubbish. What do you know of Peter the Great and Catherine? Well, then, tell me."

I would tell him. After I had finished speaking, I would wait for him to say:

"These idiots…"

And sure enough he would say:

"These idiots are teaching you falsehoods."

"Why falsehoods?"

"Because they're idiots," said Uncle Vitaly with conviction. "They think it'll do you good to have the false idea that Russia's history is a succession of righteous and intelligent monarchs. But what you're learning is some sugar-coated mythology that they've substituted for historical fact. And so you're being swindled. In any case, you'd wind up a fool, even if you learnt the real history."

"I'd definitely wind up a fool?"

"Without a shadow of a doubt. Everybody does."

"What about you?"

"Don't be insolent," he replied with absolute composure. "It isn't proper to ask such questions of one's elders. But if you really must know, I too take my place among fools, although I wish it had turned out differently."

"What's to be done, then?"

"Be a scoundrel," he said sharply, before turning away.

His had been an unfortunate marriage. He was almost totally cut off from his family and knew well that his wife, a very beautiful lady from Moscow, was unfaithful to him;

he was a great deal older than she. I would turn up in Kislovodsk every summer and always find Uncle Vitaly there—that is, until I was driven out of the Caucasus by the manoeuvres of various Bolshevik and anti-Bolshevik forces up and down the Don and across the Kuban. A year before I left Russia, while the Civil War was raging, I went there again and saw on the terrace of our dacha the hunched figure of Uncle Vitaly in his chair for one last time. He had aged since my last visit: his hair was now grey and his face gloomier than before. As I greeted him, I said: "I met Alexandra Pavlovna in the park." (This was his wife.) "She looked radiant." Uncle Vitaly cast me a sullen look.

"Do you remember Pushkin's epigrams?"

"I do."

He recited:

> *There's none like you upon the earth,*
> *The world insists, and I affirm it:*
> *While others age in line to time,*
> *Yet you grow younger every year.*

"You don't seem too happy, Uncle."

"What's to be done? My boy, I'm an old pessimist. They tell me you want to enlist."

"I do."

"What a foolish thing to do."

"And why's that?"

I thought he would begin: "These idiots…" But he didn't. He only lowered his head and said:

"Because the volunteers will lose the war."

The notion of whether the volunteers would win or lose the war didn't much interest me. I wanted to know what war was; it was that same longing I had for everything new and unknown. I joined the White Army because I happened to find myself on its territory, because it was the done thing; and if in those days Kislovodsk had been taken over by the Reds, then quite likely I would have joined the Red Army. Yet it surprised me that Uncle Vitaly, an old officer, should have reacted with such disapproval. I didn't then fully understand that Uncle Vitaly was too clever for all this and didn't attach to his officer's rank the importance that one usually does. Nevertheless, I asked him why he thought so. Looking at me with indifference, he said that they—that is, those who commanded the anti-governmental forces—didn't understand the laws of social relations. "Out there," he said, growing animated, "out there is all of starving northern Russia. Out there, my boy, is the *muzhik*. Do you know that Russia is a peasant land, or didn't they teach you this in your history?"

"I know it," I answered him.

Then Uncle Vitaly continued: "Russia," he said, "is entering the peasant stage of history, its might is the *muzhik*, and the *muzhik* serves the Red Army." The Whites, according to Uncle Vitaly's scornful observation, lacked even the romanticism that might have made war an attractive prospect; the White Army was the army of the middle classes and the quasi-intelligentsia. "It's chock-full of cocaine addicts, madmen, cavalry officers mincing like cocottes," Uncle Vitaly said sharply, "failed careerists and sergeant majors in generals' epaulettes."

"You always rail against everything," I observed. "Alexandra Pavlovna says that it's your *profession de foi*."

"Alexandra Pavlovna, Alexandra Pavlovna," said Uncle Vitaly with sudden exasperation. "*Profession de foi*—what nonsense! For twenty-five years, every day and from every quarter, I've heard this preposterous rejoinder: you always rail against everything. Just because I turn my mind to something. I lay out the reasons for the inevitable outcome of the war, and you tell me: you always rail against everything. What are you, a man or Aunt Zhenya? I reproached Alexandra Pavlovna for always reading that cheap trash, and she too told me that I was just railing against everything, as usual. No, not everything. As God is my witness, I know and love literature better than my wife does. If I curse something, I have good reason for it. You'll grow to understand," said Uncle Vitaly, raising his head, "that of everything done in any area—be it reform, reorganization of the army or an attempt to introduce new methods in education, or art, or literature—nine times out of ten it won't work. That's just the way of it. So why am I to blame if Aunt Zhenya doesn't understand this?" He paused for a minute before asking abruptly:

"How old are you?"

"I'll be sixteen in two months."

"And the devil himself is leading you to war?"

"Yes."

"But why, really, do you want to go and fight?" Uncle Vitaly suddenly uttered in astonishment. I didn't know what to say, faltered and, finally, ventured uncertainly:

"I consider it to be my duty, all the same."

"I thought more highly of you," Uncle Vitaly said disappointedly. "If your father were alive today, your words would give him no cause to rejoice."

"Why's that?"

"Now see here, my dear boy," said Uncle Vitaly with sudden tenderness. "Try to understand. Two sides are at war: the Whites and the Reds. The Whites are trying to return Russia to the historical condition she has just left. The Reds are plunging her into such chaos, the likes of which she hasn't seen since the time of Tsar Alexis."

"The end of the Time of Troubles," I murmured.

"Quite so, the end of the Time of Troubles. I see school hasn't been a complete waste of time after all." And so Uncle Vitaly set forth his views on the events of those times. He said that social categories—these words struck me unexpectedly, for I could not forget that Uncle Vitaly was an officer of the Dragoon Guards—were subordinated to the laws of some non-material biology, and that this concept was, though not always infallible, often applicable to a variety of social phenomena. "They are born, grow and die," Uncle Vitaly said, "and they don't even really die, but rather die off, like coral. Do you remember how coral islands are formed?"

"I do," I said. "I remember how they form. I even remember their red curves surrounded by the white spume of the ocean. It's really quite beautiful. I saw an illustration of it in one of Father's books."

"A process of the very same order occurs in history," Uncle Vitaly continued. "One thing dies off and another is born. Thus, to put it crudely, the Whites are like dying coral, on the dead body of which new formations are growing. It is the Reds that are growing."

"Very well, let's suppose this is so," I said. Uncle Vitaly's eyes had regained their habitual expression of mockery. "Doesn't it seem to you that truth is on the side of the Whites?"

"Truth? What truth? In the sense that they're right in attempting to seize power?"

"You could put it that way," I said, even though I thought otherwise.

"Yes, of course. But the Reds are also right, and the Greens too, and if there were Oranges and Violets into the bargain, they would be equally right."

"Anyway, the front is already at Oryol, and Kolchak's forces are headed for the Volga."

"That doesn't mean a thing. If you're still alive after all this butchery is done, you'll read in specialist books detailed accounts of the heroic defeat of the Whites and the ignominious accidental victory of the Reds—if the book is written by a scholar sympathetic to the Whites—and of the heroic victory of the workers' army over the bourgeois mercenaries—if the author is on the side of the Reds."

I answered that I was still going to fight for the Whites, since they were losing.

"That's schoolboy sentimentalism," said Uncle Vitaly with forbearance. "All right, I'll tell you what I think. Not what can come of analysing the forces directing today's events, but my own perspective on it. Don't forget, I'm an officer and a conservative in a certain sense, and, on top of all that, a man with an almost feudal conception of justice and honour."

"What do you think?"

He sighed.

"Truth is on the side of the Reds."

That evening he invited me to take a stroll with him to the park. We walked down the red alleys, past the limpid little stream and miniature grottos, under the tall, ancient trees. It grew dark, the stream sobbed and babbled; and for me that quiet noise is now mingled with the memory of our leisurely walk on the sand, the lights of the restaurant visible in the distance, and looking down and seeing my white summer trousers and Uncle Vitaly's tall boots. He was more loquacious than usual, and I could no longer hear the customary tone of irony in his voice. He was talking seriously and plainly.

"So, you're leaving us, Nikolai," he said as we delved deeper into the park. "Do you hear the babbling of that stream?" he said suddenly, interrupting himself. I listened: through the steady noise I could make out several babblings, simultaneous yet distinct from one another.

"It's the queerest thing," said Uncle Vitaly. "Why should this sound move me so? Whenever I hear it, even after all these years, it always seems to me that I'm hearing it for the first time. But that isn't what I wanted to say."

"I'm listening."

"You and I shall very likely never meet again," he said. "Either you'll be killed, or you'll wind up God only knows where, or else I'll die a natural death, waiting to see the day of your return. Each of these is equally possible."

"Why take such a dismal view of it?" I asked. Scarcely could I manage to grasp what was happening to me at any given moment, let alone imagine events far in advance; this was why all speculation about what might happen at some vague point in the future seemed absurd to me. Uncle Vitaly told me that in his youth he had been the same, but five years of solitary confinement, which had nourished his fantasy only with thoughts of the future, had amplified it to terrific proportions. In discussing some event which in his opinion was bound to happen soon, Uncle Vitaly would see at once its many facets, and his sophisticated imagination would experience an accurate premonition of its elusive psychological shell and that of the external conditions in which it might take place. More than that, his knowledge of people and the reasons propelling them to act in one way or another was incomparably richer than that typical of a man of his age; and this afforded him at first glance that almost unfathomable ability to divine, a thing that I have observed only among my few and for some reason always accidental acquaintances. Uncle Vitaly, however, almost never put this ability to use, for he was disdainfully indifferent to the fate even of his nearest relatives—and his kindness and charity could be explained, as I saw it, by an indiscriminate and near-infallible lack of sympathy.

"I loved your father dearly," Uncle Vitaly said, without answering my question. "Even if he did always laugh at my being an officer and a cavalryman. Then again, maybe he was right to laugh. I love you, too, you know," he continued. "So before you go, I want to tell you one thing. And you'd better be paying attention."

I had no idea what Uncle Vitaly wanted to tell me; in my relationship with him there was somehow no room for the notion that he could take an interest in me and advise me on anything: he always preferred to upbraid me for my failure to comprehend something or for my love of discussing abstract things, which, according to him, I didn't understand. He once laughed very nearly to the point of tears when I told him that I'd read Stirner and Kropotkin. On another occasion, he shook his head despairingly when he learnt of my penchant for the art of Victor Hugo; he spoke scornfully of this man who, as he put it, had the manners of a fireman, the soul of a sentimental fool and the grandiloquence of a Russian telegraph operator.

"Now listen here," Uncle Vitaly was saying meanwhile. "In the very near future you're going to witness a great many atrocities. You'll see what it is to kill people, to hang them, to stand them before a firing squad. None of this is new, important or even especially interesting. But here's my advice to you: never become a man of conviction, don't draw conclusions, don't reason. Try to be as simple as possible. And remember, the greatest happiness on earth is to think that you've understood something of the life around you. You won't understand it: you'll only think you understand it. And when you look back on this in the fullness of time, you'll see you were wrong. And after another year or two has passed, you'll be convinced that you were wrong the second time as well. And so on without end. But still, this is the most important and the most interesting thing that life has to offer."

"Very well," I said. "But what meaning is there in continually being wrong?…"

"Meaning?" said Uncle Vitaly, astonished. "Truly, there is no meaning, none at all—nor is one necessary."

"That can't be so. There's the law of expediency."

"No, my dear boy, meaning is a fiction, and expediency is also a fiction. Look at it this way: if you take a score of events and start to analyse them, of course you'll see that there are forces guiding their movement; but the concept of 'meaning' figures neither in these forces, nor in these movements. Take any historical fact that was the result of lengthy political manoeuvring and had an altogether definite aim. You'll see that from the vantage of achieving this aim and this aim only, such a fact cannot have meaning, because simultaneously and for seemingly the very same reasons other events have occurred, ones that were utterly unforeseen and changed everything entirely."

He looked at me as we walked between two rows of trees, and it was so dark that I almost couldn't make out his face.

"The word 'meaning'," Uncle Vitaly continued, "would cease to be a fiction only if we possessed exact knowledge that when we do one thing and not another, a certain outcome is bound to follow. If this is not always possible even in primitive mechanical sciences with specific goals in mind and under fully controlled conditions, then how can you expect it to be a certainty in the realm of social relations, the nature of which we do not understand, or in the province of individual psychology, of whose laws we are practically ignorant? There is no meaning, my dear Kolya."

"What about the meaning of life?"

Uncle Vitaly suddenly paused, as though something held him back. It was pitch dark, and I could barely make out the sky through the leaves on the trees. The animation of the park and the town remained far below; to the left the Romanovsky mountain, covered in firs, showed blue. It looked blue to me, but then, in the darkness, my eyes ought to have seen black. But I was so used to looking at the mountain in the daylight, when it really was blue, whereas in the evening I would use my vision only to trace its outline, while its blue colour was filled in by my imagination—despite the laws of light and distance. The air was very pure and fresh, and once again, as always amid the silence, a drawn-out sound that grew ever more distinct reached me from afar and died overhead.

"The meaning of life?" Uncle Vitaly repeated mournfully. I heard tears in his voice and could not quite believe my ears; I had always thought that they were unknown to this courageous and indifferent man.

"I once had a comrade who also asked me about the meaning of life," Uncle Vitaly said, "before he shot himself. He was a great comrade, a very dear comrade," he said, repeating the word "comrade" and seeming to find some illusive consolation in the fact that, resounding in the still air of the deserted park, this word sounded now just as it had done all those years ago. "He was a student at the time, and I was a junker. He was always asking me: 'What is this terrible meaningless of existence for, this knowledge that if I die an old man, repulsive to everyone, that this is somehow a good thing? Where is the sense in that? Why live only to go through that? None of us shall cheat death, you know, Vitaly. There's no salvation.' None!" cried Uncle Vitaly. "He went on: 'Why bother to be an engineer, or a lawyer, or a writer, or an officer? Wherefore this humiliation, this shame, this villainy and cowardice?' I told him then that it was possible to exist beyond such questions: 'Live, eat beefsteaks, make love, grieve over the betrayals of women, and be happy. And may God keep you from the thought of why you're doing any of it.' But he wouldn't listen, and he put a bullet through his brain. Now you ask me the meaning of life. I don't know. I just don't know."

That evening we returned home very late; and when the weary maid served us tea on the terrace, Vitaly looked at his glass, raised it, gazed though the liquid at the electric lamp—and laughed for a long while without uttering so much as a word. He muttered mockingly: the meaning of life! Then suddenly he frowned and glowered and went up to bed without wishing me goodnight.

A little later, as I was leaving Kislovodsk for the Ukraine, where I intended to enlist, Uncle Vitaly bid me a calm and cold farewell, and again in his eyes I saw that perpetual expression of indifference, ready at any moment to metamorphose into disdain. I, for one, was sorry to be leaving, for I truly did love him—whereas those around him feared him and cared little for him. "A heart of stone," his wife was wont to say of him. "A cruel man," my aunt said. "Nothing is sacred for him," his daughter-in-law echoed. None of them knew the real Uncle Vitaly. Much later, as I ruminated on his dismal life and unfortunate end, I lamented that a man of such considerable talents, with such a live and quick intellect, had squandered his life. Not even one of his relatives regretted his passing. As I said my goodbyes, I knew that I was unlikely ever to see this man again; I wanted to embrace him and bid him farewell, as I would a friend and not simply an acquaintance who had turned up at the station to see me off. But Uncle Vitaly conducted himself in a very official manner, and when, with a flick of the fingers, he brushed a bit of fluff off his sleeve, from this single gesture I understood that to say goodbye as I had wanted would have been absurd and *ridicule*. He shook my hand, and I left. It was late autumn, and in the cool air I could feel the sorrow and regret characteristic of every departure. Never could I accustom myself to this feeling: for me, every departure marked the beginning of a new existence, and consequently the necessity of living again by touch, of searching out among the new people and things that surrounded me a more or less intimate environment in which to recapture my former calm, so needed in order to make space for those internal shocks and vibrations that so singularly obsessed me. Yet at the same time I also felt sorry to be leaving the towns in which I had lived and the people whom I had come to know—for these towns and people would never be repeated in my lifetime; their simple lifelike stasis and the sharpness of their everlastingly fixed images were so unlike the other countries, towns and people that lived in my imagination, summoned by me into existence and action. Over some I had the power of destruction and creation, while over others only my memory, my impotent knowledge lingered. And this knowledge was insufficient even for divination, which gift Uncle Vitaly had possessed. For a little while longer I saw his figure on the platform, but Kislovodsk had already begun to disappear, and the sounds issuing from the station were drowned out by the iron roar of the locomotive. By the time that I reached the city where I had

GAITO GAZDANOV

lived and studied during the winter, I saw that snow was falling, flickering in the light of the street lamps. In the streets demon drivers cried out, trams thundered by, and the brightly lit windows of houses flew past, skipping over the broad, wadded back of the cabby, who would throw up his elbows as he cracked the reins with haphazard, fitful movements, just like the jerking arms and legs of a wooden toy clown. I spent a week in that city before my dispatch to the front; I passed the time visiting theatres and cabarets and crowded restaurants with Rumanian bands. On the eve of the day for which my departure was set, I bumped into Shchur, my classmate from the gymnasium; he was amazed to see me in a military uniform. "You're not joining the volunteers, are you?" he asked. And when I replied that I was, he looked at me in even greater astonishment.

"What on earth are you playing at? Have you lost your senses? Stay here, the volunteers are retreating; in two weeks our guys will be in the city."

"No, I've made my decision to go."

"Well, aren't you a rum sort. You'll live to regret it."

"I'm going, all the same."

He firmly shook my hand. "Well, I hope you won't be disappointed."

"Thanks, I don't believe I will."

"Do you really expect the volunteers to win?"

"No, not at all; that's why I won't be disappointed."

In the evening I said my farewells to Mother. My leaving came as a terrible blow to her. She begged me not to go; I had to summon all the cruelty of my sixteen years in order to leave her alone and go off to war—without conviction, without enthusiasm, solely out of a desire to see war at last and understand such new things as might regenerate me. "Fate has taken away my husband and daughters," Mother said to me. "You're all I have left, and now you're leaving." I said nothing. "It would have pained your father terribly," Mother went on, "to learn that his Nikolai was enlisting in the army of men he despised all his life."

"Uncle Vitaly told me exactly the same thing," I replied. "Don't worry, Mama, soon the war will be over and I'll be home again."

"And if it's your corpse they bring me?"

"They won't, I know it. I shan't be killed." She stood by the door to the hallway and looked at me in silence, slowly closing and opening her eyes, like one coming to her senses after a fainting fit. I picked up my suitcase; one of its clasps caught on the hem of my coat, and, seeing that I was having trouble undoing it, Mother suddenly smiled: and it was so unexpected—for she rarely smiled, even when others did. Naturally, it wasn't the snagged hem of my coat that made her smile; there were so many different emotions mixed up in this—regret, the knowledge that it was now impossible to avert my departure, the presentiment of loneliness, the memories of my father's and sisters' deaths, the shame she felt on account of the tears welling in her eyes, her love for me, and all that long life which had bound me to her from birth until that very day, when Ekaterina Genrikhovna Voronina, who was present at our farewell, suddenly buried her face in her hands and began to weep. When finally the door had closed behind me and the thought struck me that I might never again cross that threshold, that never again would Mother make the sign of the cross over me as she had just done, I wanted to turn back and stay. But it was too late, the moment for that had already passed; I was already out in the street. As I stepped outside, everything that had been my life until then was now put behind me and continued to exist without me; I no longer had any place there. It was as if my very being had vanished. Much later I would also recall that it had been snowing that evening, blanketing the street. After two days of travelling I reached Sinelnikovo; there I found the armoured train *Smoke*, which took me on as a soldier in the artillery detail. This was at the end of 1919. That winter I stopped being the schoolboy Sosedov who had just entered the seventh year; I stopped reading books, skiing, practising gymnastics, going to Kislovodsk and seeing Claire; and everything that I had done until then became but a figment of my memory. Yet even to this new life I brought my long-established habits and peculiarities: just as at home or at school significant events would often leave me cold, while trifles that, on the face of it, didn't warrant any attention were particularly important to me—so too during the Civil War all the battles and killings and casualties passed me by almost without trace, while only a handful of thoughts and emotions, for the most part far removed from those one usually has about war, remained with me forever. My fondest memory from those days is of being dispatched to an observation post at the top of a tree in a forest—and left there alone, while the armoured train went back several versts to take on water. It was the month of September, and the leaves were already turning yellow. Enemy artillery was bombarding the edge of the forest, where the observation point was located, and shells went flying over the trees with a phenomenal roar and drone—something that never happens when a shell passes over a field. The wind was blowing and the tops of the trees were swaying; a little squirrel with lively eyes, chewing something with those comical, rapid jaw movements peculiar to rodents, suddenly spotted me, took fright and instantly jumped across to the neighbouring tree, straightening out its fluffy ginger tail and for a moment remaining suspended in mid-air. The battery that was shelling the forest stood quite a distance away, and I saw only the dim red flashes that issued from the guns with each salvo. The leaves were rustling in the wind; from down below came the chirping of a grasshopper that had appeared from Lord knows where, and suddenly it fell silent, as if someone were stopping its mouth with the palm of his hand. It was so lovely and clear; all these sounds washed over me so distinctly; and in the little lake that I could see below, the rippling water was so radiant that I forgot all about having to follow the explosions and manoeuvres of enemy cavalry, whose presence reconnaissance had communicated to us, and about the fact that Russia was in the grip of civil war, and that I was taking part in it.

It was during the war that I first encountered such strange conditions and behaviour that in all likelihood I should never have seen in any other circumstances. Above all I observed the most terrible cowardice, yet I never felt in the least bit sorry for those who experienced it. I couldn't fathom how it was possible for a twenty-five-year-old to weep with fear, a soldier who, during heavy bombardment and after three six-inch shells hit the armoured platform we were manning, destroying its iron walls and wounding several people, went crawling on the floor, crying, and shouting in a piercing voice: O God, O Mummy!—while he gripped the legs of others who had managed to maintain their composure. Nor could I fathom why his fear suddenly infected the officer in command of the platform, a man who was usually very courageous, who called out to the engine driver: reverse, full steam!—although there was no new danger and the shells of the enemy artillery continued to miss the armoured train. I cannot say that in the heat of battle I never experienced fear, but mine was a feeling that easily gave way to reason; and since there was no sensuality or lure to this feeling, it was not difficult to overcome it. Aside from this, there was yet another factor that came into play: in those days—just as before and afterwards—I still lacked the ability to react immediately to my circumstances. This ability surfaced in me exceedingly rarely, and only when what I saw coincided with my inner state of being; these were for the most part situations presenting a certain degree of fixity and, in any case, having little to do with me personally; they could never have aroused my personal interest. It could have been the slow flight of an enormous bird, or someone's distant whistle, or an unexpected bend in the road, around which lay reeds and swamps, or the human-like eyes of a tamed bear, or being awoken amid the darkness of a stifling summer's night by the sudden cry of an unknown beast. But in all these cases, when it was my own fate that was at stake, or when danger threatened, what was most in evidence was that peculiar deafness of mine, which developed as a result of that same spiritual inability to react immediately to my environment. It divorced me from the ordinary world of alarm and enthusiasm that characterizes any combat situation and causes mental turmoil. For many, this mental turmoil proves overwhelming—for the cowardly and the brave alike. But I found that simple folk, peasants and agricultural workers, were especially susceptible: both bravery and fear expressed themselves more violently in them than in anyone else and reached an equal degree of desperation—in some cases calm, in others hysterical—as though they were one and the same emotion, only steered in different directions. Those who were most cowardly feared death because the power of their blind attachment to life was so uncommonly fierce; those who didn't fear it were also possessed of the very same strange life force, for only someone of great spiritual strength can be courageous. Yet this mysterious power was invested in forms that were as unalike one another as the lives of parasites and those on whom they feed. And because, on the one hand, everyone whom I had known and observed among my former tutors and acquaintances had all my life instilled in me a hatred of cowardice and a duty of courage—and never had I questioned this—and because, on the other hand, my scant intellect found it impossible to conceive of a coward's mental state, and because I had a dearth of emotional experience in which I might have found similar such sentiments, I treated these men with a disgust that grew especially severe in those cases in which the cowards were not soldiers but officers. I saw how one of them, during a period of intense fighting, instead of commanding the machine-gunners, cowered under a pile of sheepskin coats that was lying in the middle of the platform, how he blocked his ears with his fingers and did not get up until the battle was done. Another time the machine-gunners' second-in-command also hit the deck, covering his face with the palms of his hands, and although it was winter and the iron floor was terribly cold (his fingers very nearly stuck together), he lay there for almost two hours without even catching a chill—quite possibly because the monumental effect of fear had created for him some kind of temporary immunity. The third instance occurred when enemy aircraft appeared over the base—this was the name we gave to the train that accommodated soldiers and officers arriving from the front to be relieved, for there were two shifts, one on the front line, the other in the rear; they alternated every fortnight. In addition to these, there was an entire non-combatant section—that is, the soldiers who worked in the mess, the officers occupying administrative and managerial posts, officers' wives, clerks, quartermasters, and twenty or so women who were listed as laundry girls, dishwashers and cleaners in the officers' carriages; these were the sundry women who had been selected at different stations and had been seduced by the comfort of the base, the warm carriages, the electricity, the cleanliness, the abundance of food, and the pay they received for a few light duties and especially for the purely feminine favours that were asked of them. Thus, when enemy aircraft appeared and began dropping bombs over the base—which stood, as always, forty versts from the front line—Lieutenant Borshchov, the armoured train's sergeant major, looked up at the sky with a gasp, hastily crossed himself and crawled on all fours under the carriage, not in the least ashamed that those around him might see this. Just then, the porter Mikhutin, a sly *muzhik* and a thief, who had never before seen battle, leapt down from one of the cars; he jumped off the footboard and, without even looking around, set out across the field to a water tower, quickly ducking inside it. Not one of the bombs hit the base, as might have been expected; in fact, the only bomb that did cause any damage destroyed a part of that very water tower in which Mikhutin had taken cover. Granted, he was not maimed in the incident, but he took a good pounding from the falling masonry: his fat face with its sullen, swinish expression was black and blue, his clothes were doused with limewash, and when he returned looking like this, everybody laughed—not that it shamed him in the least, of course, because his sense of fear was insuperable. Another soldier, Tiyanov, a broad-shouldered chap who could easily cross himself while holding a two-*pood* kettlebell, was so faint-hearted that when he first went to the front and heard the distant cannon fire, he leapt a *sazhen* and a half from a platform and wanted to run back to the base, but couldn't because he had dislocated his leg; he was terribly glad of the dislocated leg, though, since it promised to spare him the front line. That same man once during a bombardment— he ended up having to go to the front after all—fainted and lay there with a pale face, not flinching; yet when I happened to catch him unawares, I saw him quickly open his eyes, take a look around and immediately close them again. But alongside such people I saw others too. Colonel Richter, the commander of the armoured train

Smoke, was lying, as I recall, on the roof of the carriage between two rows of screws that were used to fasten separate plates of the armour. Skidding along the iron with a shriek, an enemy shell tore off all the fastenings to the left of the colonel; he didn't even turn around; his face remained unmoved, and I didn't mark even the slightest effort on his part to maintain composure. One time the artillery detail's senior officer, Lieutenant Osipov, having climbed down from the platform in order to inspect our position from a nearby field, found himself between two chains of infantry soldiers—Reds on one side, Whites on the other. Both sides, not knowing who he was—the Reds took him for a White, and the Whites for a Red—began firing at him, and from the platform we saw columns of dust go shooting up by the second beside his legs. He just kept pressing ahead, paying no heed to the bullets; then he turned back and one bullet grazed his arm. In the heat of combat, the soldier Filippenko would softly sing Ukrainian folk songs and try to carry on a leisurely conversation with the others; he was grieved and surprised to hear curses and profanity in response. He understood neither the nervous excitement that gripped people nor their fear. "Aren't you afraid, Filippenko?" asked his commanding officer. "What's there to be afraid of?" Filippenko replied in astonishment. "Night-time in a cemetery, now that's scary. But during the day there's nothing to fear." One of the most courageous people I ever laid eyes on was the soldier Danil Zhivin, whom everyone called Danko. He was a kind-hearted slip of a man, a great lover of laughter and a good comrade. He was so lacking in ambition and so disposed to put himself out for the sake of others that it was incredible. He had survived a great many adventures, had served in every army that took part in the Civil War—the Reds, the Whites, Makhno's men, Hetman Skoropadsky's men, Petlyura's men, and even in the Social Revolutionary Sablin's unit, which lasted a matter of days. His tour of duty on board the armoured train was interrupted when he was captured by Makhno's army—together with the entire company that was fighting on the front that day. The Makhnovites assigned him to a special detachment of infantrymen guarding a bridge across the Dnieper.

The bridge, which was about a verst and three-quarters across, was occupied on one side by Makhno's forces, and on the other by the Whites. At both ends stood machine guns aimed at one another. Danko, who found himself in the sentry post on Makhno's side, decided to make his way back to the armoured train. He dispatched the relief sentry to the dugout, slung his gun over his shoulder and set off across the bridge in the direction of the volunteers, who immediately opened ferocious fire. In spite of this, Danko continued to advance as though he were walking not along a narrow strip pierced by dozens of bullets per second, but along a peaceful Russian highway leading from, say, Tula to Oryol. The relief sentry, alarmed by this unexpected firing, came running out of the dugout and, seeing Danko's retreating figure, also opened fire on him from a second gun. Danko crossed the bridge without so much as a scratch. He was arrested by the Whites, and some foolish infantry officers—two staff captains—took him for a spy and wanted to put him up against the wall. Danko rained down on them terrible curses, invoking the Lord God and the Apostles; this would all have been to no avail had not his comrades from the armoured train come to find out what was going on. Lieutenant Osipov arrived to see the ragged Danko screaming at the infantry officers and brandishing both his revolver and his rifle. After the intervention of the officer from the armoured train, they let him go, saying that they had never seen such an undisciplined soldier. "You can take your discipline and ——!" shouted Danko. "How is it that you weren't afraid, Danko?" they asked him after he had changed and been fed and was sitting by the stove in the heated freight car, smoking a cigarette made of Stamboul tobacco. "Who wasn't afraid?" replied Danko. "Oh, I was afraid all right." Another time Danko, having been sent on reconnaissance, wound up being taken prisoner again, all because he landed in a village that had been captured by the Reds: having entered one of the huts there, he began to joke with the mistress and enquired whether there were Bolsheviks in the village—just moments before three Red Army soldiers appeared out of nowhere. Danko didn't even have time to reach for his rifle. They disarmed him, imprisoned him in a shed, posted a guard and sentenced Danko to death. And even then, three days later, having tracked down the base of the armoured train, which in the meantime had retreated a distance of sixty versts, Danko showed up as if nothing had happened. I was present during his debriefing with the commander.

"Where were you, Danko?"

"I was taken prisoner."

"And just how were you taken prisoner?"

"The Reds arrested me."

"And they didn't do anything to you?"

"No, but they were going to shoot me."

"So what did you do?"

"I ran away."

"And how did you manage that?"

"I killed the sentry and made a run for it."

"And they didn't catch you?"

"No," said Danko, "I ran like hell." He laughed. To me the very thought that Danko could have killed the sentry seemed strange and out of character. In all likelihood he had simply found no alternative; and, of course, the instinct for self-preservation would have drowned out his capacity for reflection—whether to kill the sentry or not. Were it not for this instinct, Danko would have died long ago. He was, as the soldiers said of him, very young and happy-go-lucky: he once reduced an entire company to laughter when he went chasing after a little white piglet that he had bought somewhere; for a long time he ran after it, screaming at it and trying to catch it with his cap; he whistled for it, flailing his arms as he ran, and we watched until both he and the piglet had vanished from sight. That evening he returned with a pig in tow, which he had somehow managed to swap for the piglet. The men joked that Danko had been chasing the piglet for so long that in the meantime it had grown up. Danko laughed, holding his cap and looking at the floor. He was a jolly, infinitely good-natured and infinitely desperate man.

"Danko, would you ever go to the North Pole?" I asked.

"Is it interesting there?"

"Very interesting, and there are lots of polar bears."

"Oh, no," he said, "I'm afraid of bears."

"Why on earth are you afraid of them? They can't sentence you to death."

"But they can bite you," he replied with a laugh.

He could never quite kick the habit of addressing me formally. "Danko," I explained to him, "you're a soldier, like me. Why must you always be so formal? You can talk to me as you do to Ivan." (This was his buddy.) "I can't," Danko replied, "I'd be too ashamed." This Ivan, a sharp-witted Ukrainian, a cool-headed and courageous soldier, once asked me:

"What is the Milky Way?"

"What's it to you all of a sudden?"

"The boys were asking me, 'Ivan, what's that up there in the sky, like milk?' I told them it's the Milky Way. But as for what the Milky Way is, I don't know." I explained it to him as best I could. The very next day he came to me again:

"Can you please tell me what the length of a circumference is equal to?"

"It's determined by a special mathematical equation," I said. "I don't know if you'll understand the terminology." I gave him the equation for the length of a circumference.

"Ah-ha," he confirmed with a satisfied air. "I was testing you. I thought you might not know it. I asked Volunteer Svirsky earlier, then I wrote it down and came to test you."

He was a superb storyteller; I never met anyone among so-called "intellectuals" who could hold a candle to him. He was devilishly clever and observant, and possessed the creative gift of being able to see the funny side of life, without which humour always falls a little flat. I cannot remember the stories in which Ivan revealed his astounding talent for mimicry: since his art was so easy and of the moment, it hardly lent itself to a lasting impression. These days I can remember only his account of a conversation that he had with a Red general, when some old nags had been sent to a battery of which Ivan was then in charge. "So I tell him," Ivan would say, "'Comrade Commander, do these look like horses to you? They're going around and look surprised that they haven't keeled over yet.' And he replies: 'I thank the top brass that not all of my commanders are as capricious as those old nags.' And I say to him: 'God forbid you should kick the bucket, Comrade Commander. We couldn't very well use those horses for fear you'd lurch around too much.'"

I spent my time with soldiers, but they were somewhat wary of me because I didn't understand a great many things that were, as far as they were concerned, extraordinarily simple; at the same time, they thought I knew things that were in turn inaccessible to them. I was ignorant of the words they used; they would laugh at me if I said "to draw water": "What's the use drawing it if you can't drink it?" they would quip. Nor did I have the knack for talking to peasants; in their eyes I was forever some sort of home-grown foreigner. Once the platform commander instructed me to go to the village to buy a pig. "I ought to warn you," I said, "that I've never bought a pig before in my life. If I don't get the right thing, then on your head be it."

"What's all this?" he replied. "It's just buying a pig, not Newton's binomial theorem or some such. No great wisdom needed."

And so I set out for the village. In every hut I entered, I was regarded with incredulity and contempt. "You wouldn't happen to have a pig for sale, would you?" I would ask.

"A what?"

"A pig."

"No, no pigs."

I must have gone around forty yards and returned to the platform empty-handed. "I've come to the conclusion," I told the officer, "that this particular variety of mammal is unknown in these parts."

"And I've come to the conclusion that you simply don't know how to buy a pig," he retorted. I put up no argument; and then Ivan, who had been present throughout the whole conversation, offered me his services. "Come with me," he said, "and we'll buy ourselves a pig in no time." I shrugged and set out again for the village. In the very first hut—the same in which I had been told that there were no pigs—Ivan bought an enormous hog for pennies. Prior to the purchase, he spoke with the owners about the harvest, explained that his uncle, who lived in the Poltava Governorate, was a close friend and neighbour of the owner's brother-in-law, praised the cleanliness of the hut (even though the place was filthy), said that there couldn't be pigs on such a farm and asked for a drink. It all ended with our being stuffed to the gills, sold a pig and seen to the gate. "There's your binomial," I told the commander when we returned. And it was always the case that wherever I had to deal with peasants, I would have no luck whatsoever; they didn't even understand me well, since I lacked their plain speech despite wanting it dearly. On board the armoured train, however, were those who had brushed themselves down and acquired a certain polish: railway workers and telegraph operators. Our boys were very dandified, wore "free" trousers, which was a mark of freethinking, while some bedecked their fingers with rings and signets of such titanic proportions that no one doubted for an instant their being counterfeit. The greatest quantity of jewels was worn by the chief among the armoured train's miscreants, the former butcher Klimenko. He spent all his free time in a state of strained attention: he never ceased to twirl his moustaches with his left hand, while holding the right in the air, nearer to his eyes, all the better to see the glitter of his rings. His vices became public knowledge after he was caught with money that he'd stolen from his neighbour, after which the commander said to him: "Well now, Klimenko, you have a choice: either I put you on trial and have you shot like a dog, or else I have all the men lined up to watch me strike you square in the face a few times." Klimenko fell to his knees and begged the commander to strike him in the face. In fact his own words were "in the mug". This was done promptly the following morning; afterwards, on the train, Klimenko would often recall the ordeal and say: "I can only laugh at the commander's stupidity"—and truly he did laugh. The second miscreant, Valentin Alexandrovich Vorobyov, was a former village stationmaster. As with the majority of ageing miscreants, he was exceedingly dapper: he wore a fluffy beard, which he combed with the greatest care; he was very courteous towards others, sang melancholy Ukrainian songs in a high tenor voice—and in spite of all this was the very model of a notorious out-and-out scoundrel. He could stitch up a comrade and see him tried, could rob his neighbour like Klimenko, and, needless to say, in a spot of trouble he would have sold his own mother. The very day I arrived aboard the armoured train, he stole from me a box containing a thousand cigarettes. The women seemed to adore this man; he slept with all the serving girls and sweepers who found themselves in his dominion, and when one of them rebuffed him, he wrote a denunciation, accusing her of socialism, though the poor woman was illiterate. She was arrested and sent somewhere under convoy; it was winter, and she was left carrying her two-year-old little girl in her arms. As I watched Vorobyov, I often wondered why it was that women typically preferred scoundrels: perhaps, I told myself, it was because scoundrels are more distinct than the average man—a scoundrel has something about him that other men lack—and also because every, or almost every, quality, when carried to the utmost degree, ceases to be regarded as an ordinary human trait and acquires the magnetic force of exceptionalism. And so, despite the fact that my former life had ended, I hadn't quite left it all behind: I retained some habits from my schooldays—I was, after all, still a schoolboy—and my thoughts took on a certain bent, one that predisposed to idleness and inconstancy my initial observations, which consequently served as the mere pretext for my fantasy's return to its favoured places. Women love hangmen: for them, the crimes of centuries past have yet to lose their thrilling appeal, and so why not suppose that Vorobyov was but a miniature of more grandiose crimes? But this was absurd and a far cry from the reality. Vorobyov busied himself by stealing sugar and supplies from neighbouring goods trains; one night he even managed to shunt a brand-new second-class carriage away from the train belonging to the commander of the front, General Tryasunov. But in the evenings, as he lay in his bunk, his face pale from drink and his eyes bleary and full of melancholy, he lamented that the will of fate had compelled him to partake in the Civil War.

"My God!" he would say, almost with tears in his eyes. "What a state of affairs! People shot, hanged, killed, tortured. And what am I doing here? Whom did I wrong? What's it all for? O Lord, how I'd like to go home; I have a wife; the little ones ask: where's Papa? While Papa's sitting here, beneath the gallows. What am I to tell them?" he shouted. "What's my excuse? My sole consolation is that we're heading for Alexandrovsk; I'll surprise my wife in the dead of night and say: 'Are you tired of waiting, my darling? Well, here I am.'"

And truly, in Alexandrovsk Vorobyov did visit his wife and returned contented. But when we had gone forty versts and spent three days stationed at a little halt, his melancholy reappeared:

"My God, what a state of affairs! People shot, hanged. And for what?" he shouted again. "My children ask: where have you been, Papa? What am I to tell them?" He fell silent, sighed and then said pensively: "We'll soon be in Melitopol, I'll go home again and see my wife. 'Are you tired of waiting, my darling?' I'll say. 'Well, here I am.'"

"Is your wife already in Melitopol?" I enquired. He looked at me with unseeing, drunken eyes, which betrayed a look of tenderness and gratitude.

"Yes, dear friend, in Melitopol."

Yet after departing Melitopol, he continued to dream about how he would see his wife, this time as far off as Dzhankoy.

"Your wife's quite a treasure, old chap," they would mock him. "She's no wife, but the omnipresent Virgin Mary. How is it that she can be in Alexandrovsk, and in Melitopol, and in Dzhankoy? And everywhere children and an apartment? You've got a nice little arrangement there."

And so Vorobyov offered an explanation, which by all accounts seemed perfectly satisfactory to him but left the others astonished.

"Children?" he said. "Well, I am a railwayman, you know."

"What on earth does that mean?"

"You're a queer lot," Vorobyov marvelled. "Evidently you don't know what it is to work on the railways. A wife in every town, my dears, in every town."

The third miscreant was Paramonov, a student who was wounded in the leg not long before I volunteered. He never in fact caused anyone any harm, but every day, an hour or two before the doctor's rounds, he would rub butter into his wound in order to prevent it from healing; hence, he was judged unfit for duty for an infinitely long time and never did see the front. Everybody saw and knew what he was doing, but treated him with silent contempt and disgust, and not one of them had the nerve to tell him that what he was doing was wrong. He was always alone: people avoided talking to him; he usually sat in his corner, looking around furtively and eating *salo* and bread. He was a real glutton. He lived like a lonely animal whose presence is tolerated, unpleasant though it may be. He was sullen and hostile towards everyone, and when people passed by his bed, he would follow them with a look of suspicion and malevolence. They eventually dispatched him somewhere else. I remembered Paramonov several years later, when I was abroad and saw a dying eagle owl that had been bound to a tree with a tightly wound strap; no sooner had the eagle owl heard somebody's footsteps than it straightened up, its feathers bristled and it slowly flapped its wings and clacked its beak; and its cruel, unsee-ing yellow eyes looked straight ahead. On the train there were cheats and swindlers; there was even an evangelist who had come from God knows where, installed himself in our carriage and lived comfortably and without a care in the world, preaching non-resistance to evil. "I've never laid a finger on these rifles of yours, nor shall I," he would say. "It's a sin."

"And if you're attacked?"

"I'll repel them with the Word." But one day, after he had fetched himself dinner—a mess tin of borscht and another of buckwheat—only for it to be pinched from under his nose, he flew into a rage, grabbed, by a strange coincidence, that very rifle which he had sworn not to touch, and would have caused quite a tragedy had he not been disarmed. But the most remarkable man I came across during the war was the soldier Kopchik, whose outward distinction lay in his indomitable laziness. He loathed any kind of exertion and did everything with the greatest show of effort and sighing, although he was perfectly hale and hearty. The soldiers had no special liking for him on account of his continual shirking of duties; they found themselves having to pick up much of the slack for him. He always lived as if in hiding, replete with the fear that he would suddenly be made to load flour onto the wagons or carry water or peel potatoes. No sooner would he stroll past the base than his unshaven chin, teary eyes and whole figure in its dirty, frayed service jacket and equally worn-out trousers would vanish; a minute later and even the bloodhounds wouldn't be able to find him. He did his best to avoid the front for the same reason that he hid away in the base: there one had to work. But if in the rear there was still a chance of shirking this, then on the platform, in the heat of battle, the very idea was inconceivable. This soldier's laziness was so immeasurably great that it surpassed his fear of death, since he didn't entirely understand the meaning of danger; on the other hand, he knew full well that work prevented his living in idleness and dreaming—something he loved more dearly than anything on earth. I couldn't imagine a situation wherein Kopchik might suddenly reveal the least fraction of his immense energy, which he spent on thinking up ways in which to shirk every kind of work and on lengthy reposes under the wagons, as was his wont on a warm summer's day. I didn't know whether Kopchik was capable of performing even the paltriest task, one that might have indicated that he reflected on why he was alive and revealed the object of the lengthy meditations that filled his customary idleness. Then one day on the platform, during intense fighting, when with suffering in his eyes Kopchik was fishing out shells from their racks and handing them over to be loaded, each one accompanied by a plaintive sigh, and when after the fifth one he said: my back hurts, they're very heavy, these shells—an enemy projectile exploded over our gun. Wounded in the stomach, our gunner lay on the floor, and the gun stopped firing. In the immediate confusion nobody knew what to do, and only Kopchik, who saw that for the moment he no longer had to work, sighed in relief, clapped his hand on the still-hot gun and with an altered, almost bouncing gait, went over to the wounded man. Blood was flooding the floor; the final throes of death were etched on the wounded man's face. "You're not going to die," Kopchik told him amid the general silence. In the distance, at equal intervals, came the sound of four cannon shots. "Just look how healthy you are," he went on calmly. "Your blood's bright red, a sick man's blood is dark blue."

"My heart won't hold out," said the gunner.

"Your heart?" echoed Kopchik. "You're wrong there. Your heart's strong; only a weak heart couldn't take this. Now, here, I'll tell you about a weak heart. I once went to bathe my horse, and not far off I see a water sprite looking very sad." The gunner made an effort to look at Kopchik. "'Well,' I think, 'let's give him a fright.' So

I frightened him. Oh, I shouted: 'What are you doing here, whiskers?' And he died of fright, because his heart was weak. Didn't have the heart of a man, you see. But you do, your heart's good and strong." But before we could make it back to base, the gunner died; and when three days later, as I was walking along the railway bed, I saw from under the wagon Kopchik's tangle of hair, I felt strange and troubled in my soul—and I turned my back on him all the quicker: there was something inhumane and wicked about this soldier, something I wanted nothing to do with. But my attention was soon distracted by an argument that was taking place between the chief cook for the officers' assembly—which was being held in a special Pullman carriage—and the armoured train's boot-shiner, a handsome fifteen-year-old lad called Valya, who, being the lover of this no-longer-youthful, lame woman, had been unfaithful to her with either the laundress or the dishwasher; she was scolding him for this in front of a whole crowd of people, using the choicest vocabulary, and three soldiers who were standing nearby very nearly split their sides laughing. Romances with servants took up so much of the officers' time, to say nothing of the more enterprising among the soldiers. The servants were quick to understand their worth and began to put on airs, and one of them, Katyusha, a buxom girl from Yaroslavl, would neither have anything to do with anyone nor heed any words of persuasion until she had been paid up front. The armoured train's teller of salty anecdotes, Lieutenant Dergach, carped about her to anyone who would lend an ear.

"No, Mister Lieutenant," Katyusha would proudly say, "I'm not sleeping with anyone for free now. Give me that ring you're wearing and I'll sleep with you." Dergach hesitated for a long time. "You see," he would say, "this ring was a sacred gift from my fiancée"—but love, as he would say, won the day, and Lieutenant Dergach no longer has a ring, unless, that is, he has bought another since. The most unobtainable woman on board the armoured train, however, was a sister of mercy, a proud woman who treated all the soldiers with disdain and only rarely condescended to disparaging conversations with them. I remembered how, one evening, as I lay on my bunk, she was dressing Paramonov's wounds, having brought him into my compartment earlier because the electric lamp there was brighter. She lifted her head and saw my face. "You're so young," she said. "Which province are you from?"

"Petersburg, sister."

"Petersburg? How did you end up in the south?"

"I travelled here."

"What did you do before? Were you with the serving staff?"

"No, sister, I was a student."

"At a parish school, no doubt?"

"No, sister, not at a school."

"Well, where then?"

"At a gymnasium," I said and, unable to hold it in any longer, I burst out laughing.

She blushed. "What year were you in?"

"The seventh, esteemed sister."

After that she avoided me, and only observed me from afar.

Just as, in order to remember clearly and distinctly my life in the military academy and the incomparable, stony sorrow I left behind in that tall building, I had only to taste a cutlet, meat sauce or macaroni, so now, no sooner do I catch the smell of burnt-out coal than I immediately see before me the beginning of my service on the armoured train, the winter of 1919, Sinelnikovo covered in snow, the corpses of Makhnovites hanging from telegraph poles—their bodies frozen stiff, swaying in the hibernal winds and striking the wood of the poles with a light thud—the settlements looming black beyond the station, the whistles of locomotives, sounding like distress signals, and the white caps of the rails, inscrutable in their stillness. It seemed to me that they were rushing ahead, shuddering at the joints, and as if wordlessly speaking of a distant journey through the snow and the black colonies of Russia, through winter and war, into strange lands that were like enormous aquariums, full of water that you could breathe like air, and music that rippled the green surface; beneath the surface drifted the long stems of plants; behind the glass fabulous animals floated by on water lilies; I couldn't picture them, but I never ceased to feel their presence whenever I looked at the tracks and the sleepers half-covered in snow, like the boards of an infinitely long fence that somebody had knocked over. There was yet another thing that I owed to my stint on board the armoured train: a feeling of perpetual departure. The base would leave one place for another, and those objects that had constantly, statically surrounded me—my books, my clothes, a handful of etchings, the electric lamp above my head—would suddenly start to move, and so I came to understand movement, and the ruling nature of this idea, more distinctly than at any other time. I could want or not want to leave, but already the lamp would have begun to swing, already my books would begin to judder on the shelf, the carabine that was hung up on the wooden wall would now scuttle across it, and outside the snow-covered earth would go spinning while the light from the base window would quickly dash across the field, now rising, now falling, trailing behind it a long, right-angled strip, a road from one land into another. While the train gathered speed as it pulled out of the station, the contorted legs of the hanged men would fly by, their white underdrawers billowing in the wind like the sails of a ship caught in a storm. Those complex interlacings of the many reasons which had compelled me, during the winter of that year, to find myself on board an armoured train making its way south by night—reasons that have ceased to exist for good, for no memory has preserved them—have long since passed; yet this journey still continues within me and probably, until death itself comes, I shall at times feel myself lying once again on the upper bunk of my compartment, and once again, through the lit windows intersecting both space and time, I shall see flickering images of hanged men carried off under white sails into oblivion. Once again the snow will begin to whirl and that shadow of a vanished train flying through the long years of my life will begin to dance as it lurches around. And perhaps the fact that I always briefly regretted leaving people and places, perhaps this feeling of only fleeting regret was so illusive because everything I had seen and loved—soldiers, officers, women, snow and war—all this would never leave me, until the hour of my last, fatal journey, the slow descent into a black abyss, a million times longer than my earthly existence, one so long that as I fall I shall have time to forget everything I have seen, understood, felt and loved; and once I have forgotten everything that I have loved, only then shall I die.

One of my last fellow travellers to be forgotten will be Arkady Savin. He was a unique fellow, a man who resembled the people populating my imagination. The miraculous force of the twentieth century made of him a conquistador, a romantic and a bard, as though having plucked his broad-shouldered shadow from the gloomy expanses of the Middle Ages. He served with us and, just as we did, he too went to the front, but everything he did was exceptional and extraordinary. In a battle with Makhno's infantry, when only two men out of fourteen remained on the armoured train's platform—the rest had been killed or wounded—Arkady, whose jaw had been disfigured by a blast injury, stepped on the body of the first in command, whose head had been blown off—his headless body still writhing, the fingers of his already inhuman, dissociated hands still clawing at the floor—and, befouling his service jacket in human brains, Arkady manned the gun alone and for a long time, firing at the sheer mass of Makhnovite soldiers clambering onto the railway embankment. His courage was unlike any ordinary courage: all his deeds were characterized by accuracy, incredible speed and confidence. And seemingly the consciousness of his own immeasurable superiority over others never left him. His actions during moments of danger were quick, like those of a Japanese conjurer or an acrobat: on the whole there was something Asiatic about Arkady, a part of the mysterious spiritual power that is possessed by people of the yellow race and is inaccessible to whites. That being said, Arkady was also broad and heavy. The officers never could forgive him the sneers with which he met their ineffectual orders during battle. When the armoured train broke through to the front and the platform, weighing several thousand *poods*, rolled irrepressibly along the rails, trembling and thundering, Arkady's figure standing at the front and looking straight ahead—despite there being nothing surprising or out of the ordinary about this pose—looked to me like a sombre statue atop an engine of war. Thus did he appear to me on the front line. But away from the front line he was different.

He loved to dress well, drank prodigiously, and would always go into the town or village nearest to the base. At night we would be woken by the reverberations of his rich baritone; he always sang as he made his way back. He was, in point of fact, a rather good singer; he understood the true meaning of music. Pale of face and with his head inclined on his chest, he would sit absolutely still in his compartment for whole minutes at a time; and then, all of a sudden, a deep sound from his chest would fill the carriage; and a moment later I would no longer see the walls of the carriage with the rifles hung on them, nor the books, nor the lamps, nor even my comrades—as if they had never existed, as if everything I had hitherto known had been some terrible aberration, and there was nothing else in the world but this voice and Arkady's white face with its laughing eyes, although the voice sang only sorrowful songs. And then I would muse that there were no bad sorrowful songs, and that if some seemed to have bad lyrics, it was only because I was incapable of appreciating them, because I couldn't while listening to a naïve song give myself over to it wholeheartedly, couldn't forget those aesthetic habits instilled in me by my upbringing, which had neglected to teach to me the precious art of self-erasure. More often than anything else, Arkady liked to sing a romance whose verse form might at some other time have provoked only a smile from me. But if I had been able to mark the shortcomings of this form during Arkady's singing, it would surely have made me a thousand times unhappier than I was. Never again did I hear this romance anywhere or from anyone:

I'm all alone. But time so quickly gallops on,
The days, the weeks, the years rush by.
Only in dreams does joy now come;
Never in waking do we meet.

Now soon, so soon, upon life's ocean
My drifting canoe will disappear.
Ah, hear the waves of my reproach,
You'll know the loneliness that was mine.
Ah, hear the waves of my reproach,
You'll know the loneliness that was mine…

Soldiers, officers and the women of the armoured train would gather beneath the carriage windows. On summer evenings Arkady would sing, and his voice would drown in the distant, searing silence of the dark air. He sang his song even in those days when we were making our final retreat and before us the little blue lakes of the Sivash stretched out: we were leaving Taurida. Standing by the window, Arkady went on singing of his canoe, while the train sounded its whistle and its iron wheels gnashed and vanished amid clouds of stinging dust; and in their midst the plump cupolas of a church would disappear only to rise up again before us.

Arkady often dreamt, and not long before this retreat a mermaid came to him in a dream: she was laughing and beating her tail, and she swam alongside him, pressing her cold body against him, her scales glittering blindingly. I remembered Arkady's dream when, late one evening in Sebastopol, I spotted upon the autumnal waves of the Black Sea a motorboat racing towards an enormous British cruiser that was standing in the roads; it left in its tracks a glittering crest of water, and all of a sudden it seemed to me that through the foam I could hear scarcely audible laughter, and an unbearable brilliance cut through the deep blue.

For a whole year the armoured train had traversed the railways of Taurida and the Crimea, like a wild beast, driven by the pack and encircled by hunters. It changed direction, advanced, then retreated, after which it headed one way, only to race back some time later. To the south, the sea unfolded before us; to the north, armed Russia barred our way. And all around us fields went spinning in the windows, green in summer, white in winter, but always empty and hostile. The armoured train had been everywhere, and in the summer it arrived in Sebastopol. There were white lime roads passing above the sea, clay mountains towering along the shoreline, and little pochards flying hither and thither, diving headlong into the water. Rusting ironclads stood anchored at forgotten piers; by their sides, which sat deep in the water, seahorses jumped; black crabs moved sideways across the seabed, glassfish swam by as if blind, and in the dark hollows of the submarine landscape idle gobies floated motionless. It was torrid and quiet, and it seemed to me as if amid this sun-drenched stillness, above the blue sea, some transparent deity were dying in the limpid air.

That period in my life seemed to have transpired in three different countries: the land of summer, silence and the lime sultriness of Sebastopol; the land of winter, snow and blizzards; and the land of our nocturnal history, night alarms and battles, and whistles in the dark and cold. Life was different in each of these countries, and, arriving in one of them, we carried the others with us. In the chill of night, standing on the iron floor of the armoured train, I would see before me the sea and lime; sometimes in Sebastopol the brilliance of the sun, reflected on the invisible glass, would suddenly transport me to the north. But in particular it was the land of the night that was so unlike anything I had known in my life until then. I recalled how at night the mournful, drawn-out whine of bullets would pass slowly overhead; and the fact that the bullet flew very quickly, while its sound glided so leisurely and melancholically, made all this involuntary animation of the air, this frenetic, uncertain movement of sounds in the sky so especially strange. Sometimes you could hear the frantic ringing of a tocsin in a village; the flames of a fire would light up red clouds that until then had lain invisible in the darkness, and out of the houses people would come running in such alarm, the sort that sailors must feel as they run out onto the deck of a ship that has sprung a leak in the open sea, far from any shore. I often thought of ships then, as though rushing ahead of time to live out the life that was destined for me later, when I was tossed up and down on a steamer in the Black Sea, halfway between Russia and the Bosphorus.

There was a great deal of unreality in that contrived union of motley characters who manned the cannon and machine guns: they moved about the margins of southern Russia, rode on horseback, sped about on trains, perished, crushed under the wheels of retreating artillery, died and, struggling as they did, vainly attempted to fill the enormous expanse of sea, air and snow with their own ungodly meaning. And the simplest soldiers, the only ones who remained throughout this state of affairs the same old Ivanovs and Sidorovs, dreamers and idlers—these people suffered more than any others from the untruth and unnaturalness of what was going on, and perished all the sooner for it. Thus, for example, perished the armoured train's barber, Kostyuchenko, a young soldier, a drunkard and a dreamer. He would cry out in the night; he dreamt of fires, and horses, and locomotives on cogwheels. For whole days, from dawn till dusk, he would sharpen his razor, uttering cries and laughing to himself. People began to give him a wide berth. One fine day, while giving the commander of the armoured train his morning shave—soldiers were not supposed to speak in his presence—he suddenly launched into a tripping motif with the unexpectedly clipped sounds characteristic of several soldiers' songs:

> *Oi, oi!*
> *I go a-walking to the tavern,*
> *There lies a woman on her side,*
> *Asleep.*

On he wailed, never ceasing those habitual, mechanical movements as he shaved the commander's rapidly reddening cheeks. Then he set aside the razor, stuck two fingers in his mouth and began to whistle shrilly, after which he took up the razor again and cut the curtains on the window to shreds. They led him out of the commander's compartment and for a long time didn't know what to do with him. At last a decision was made—and he was forced into an empty goods wagon from one of the countless trains that brought, Lord knows why or where, the bodies of soldiers who had died of typhus and the convulsing bodies of the sick who were yet to die. The ailing lay on straw, and the wooden floor with its numerous cracks shuddered along with them; no matter where the train went, they died all the same; and, after days of travelling, the bodies of the sick made only those dead movements that came from the jolting of the train—as happened with the carcasses of horses that had been killed, or indeed other animals that had perished. And so Kostyuchenko was borne away in this empty wagon; no one ever did find out what became of him. I imagined his shining eyes amid the darkness of that tightly sealed goods wagon and, somewhere far off in the distance, the mysterial state of his dimming mind and glimmering consciousness, the sort retained by those who are mad. But Kostyuchenko's case was the last from our time on the front line. For, after the long winter, the icy blue mirrors of the Sivash and the monotony of interminable sandbanks with black sleepers, we left behind the red lights of semaphores, the round-bellied water towers of ice that for days and weeks lined our "approach to the Crimea", and, after a stop in Dzhankoy, we broke out into the country's heartland. We tarried in Dzhankoy, with its dark houses where officers' wives, like so many Messalinas, found shelter; having long been deprived of their husbands, they would come into our carriages to drink vodka and eat beefsteaks brought from the station's snack bar, and, having sated themselves, with hiccups of wearied greed they would fidget restlessly on the seats of the compartment and with quick, imperceptible movements unfasten their worn dresses and later cry and scream from passion, only moments later to cry again, though this time with more affected and transparent tears, and lament, as they said, "the good old days". This grief would suddenly paint in fantastic, festive colours their obscure lives in the provinces, married to infantry captains, drunkards and gamblers; it would seem to them that back then they hadn't realized their meagre happiness, that their lives had been happy and pleasant; indeed, they lacked the art of memory, and again and again they each of them told, always in exactly the same words, how on the night before Easter Sunday they would walk with lit candles and how the bells would peal. I never encountered such women before the war and the armoured train. They spoke in military jargon and carried themselves loosely (especially after sating their hunger), slapped men on the arm and winked at them. Their learning was astonishingly scant; a terrible spiritual poverty and a vague sense that their lives ought to have turned out differently made them unstable; as a type they most of all resembled prostitutes—but prostitutes who carried the burden of memory. Only one of these creatures—those women who are now inseparable in my memory from the soiled velvet of the divans, from the kerosene street lamps of Dzhankoy, and from the neat slices of marinated herring that were served with wine and vodka—only Elizaveta Mikhaylovna was unlike her sisters. Somehow I would always be asleep whenever she visited; she would come either around nine o'clock in the morning or around two o'clock at night. I would be roused and told: wake up, you're in the way, Elizaveta Mikhaylovna's here—and this combination of names would wake me in an instant. After a while Elizaveta Mikhaylovna became a mysterious fixture of my dreams; I would hear, "Elizaveta Mikhaylovna," then dream, then hear again, "Elizaveta Mikhaylovna," and when I opened my eyes, I would see a short, slender woman with a generous red mouth and laughing eyes, and bluish scintillations would seem to dance on the sallow skin of her face. She looked foreign. I should never have known anything about her had I not overheard, waking up one day, her conversation with one of my colleagues, the philologist Lavinov. They were discussing literature; in a cheery sing-song she was reciting verses, and by the sound of her voice it was clear that she was sitting down, rocking back and forth. Lavinov was the most educated of us: he loved Latin and often read me Caesar's commentaries, to which I listened out of politeness, for only recently I had studied them at the gymnasium—as with everything that I was forced to study, I found them dull and boring—but alongside his love for Caesar's laconic and precise language, Lavinov had a fondness for Korolenko's melancholy lyrics and even some of Kuprin's tales. Most of all, however, he loved Garshin. Yet despite such peculiar tastes, he always understood perfectly what he read—and this understanding surpassed even his own spiritual capacity; it imbued his speech with a peculiar sense of uncertainty, though his knowledge was extensive enough. In his deep voice he would say:

"Indeed, Elizaveta Mikhaylovna, that's just the way of it. It's no good."

"No good at all."

Thus the conversation would wear on—forever about what was good or not good. They seemed to lack any other words. But Elizaveta Mikhaylovna wouldn't leave; yet from her tone of voice it was apparent that, in every one of Lavinov's "goods" or "not goods", something important and having nothing at all to do with this conversation was taking place within her, something equally significant both for her and for Lavinov. It is the same when a person is drowning and bubbles appear on the surface above him; whoever does not see the drowning man go under notices only the bubbles and ascribes to them no significance, while underwater a man is choking and dying, and it is through these bubbles that all his long life, with its multitude of feelings, impressions, pities and loves, departs. The very same was happening to Elizaveta Mikhaylovna: "good" or "not good" were merely the bubbles on the surface of their conversation. Afterwards I heard her begin to cry and Lavinov speaking to her in a quavering voice; following which they both left. She never visited us again, and only just before our departure did I see her with Lavinov at the station; I sat down at a table opposite them and ate, and after my fourth pie, Elizaveta broke into peals of laughter and, turning to Lavinov, said:

"My, doesn't your sleepy friend have a fine appetite when he's awake?"

Lavinov looked at her with eyes glassy from happiness and answered "yes" to all her questions. Elizaveta Mikhaylovna was immaculately turned out; she had an air of confidence and contentment. And now, seeing that she was happy, I suddenly felt a sense of pity, as if it would have been better had she remained as she was before, when I saw her in my dreams as I woke and fell asleep, hearing this combination of names: Elizaveta Mikhaylovna; it never ceased being a woman's name, but for me it became a state of my own being, lodged between a dark dream world and the red velvet of the divans that would appear before me the moment I opened my eyes.

After Dzhankoy in winter, it was Sebastopol that rose up in my memory, covered in a stony white dust, the static verdure of Primorsky Boulevard, and the bright sand of its alleyways. Waves crash against the great slabs of the quays and, as they roll out, uncover green rocks where moss and seaweed grow; the seaweed paddles helplessly in the water, and its drooping stalks resemble the branches of a willow; ironclads stand at anchor in the roads, and the eternal landscape of the sea, the masts and the white seagulls lives and stirs, as it does wherever one finds a sea, a quay and ships, and where now there stands a stone outline of buildings raised atop a sandy yellow expanse from which the ocean retreats. In Sebastopol it was plainer than anywhere else: there was a sense that we were living out our last days in Russia. Ships sailed in and out, British and French sailors quit the shore and their ships vanished as they put out to sea, from where it seemed impossible to return to Russia. It was as if the sea had always been the gateway to our homeland, which lay far away, on maps of tropical lands with tall, erect trees and regular patches of green, while what we took to be our home—the dry heat of southern Russia, the arid fields and salty, Asiatic lakes—was but a delusion. One day I killed a pochard with my rifle; it bobbed around on the waves for a long time and always seemed to be on the verge of touching upon the shore, when the coastal tide would carry it off once again. I left only when it had grown dark and I could no longer see the pochard. With equal helplessness we, too, wavered on the surface of events; the tide of history carried us further and further away—until, having escaped Russia's gravitational pull, we were forced into the realm of other, more ancient influences and journeyed, with neither romanticism nor sail, aboard black coal ships away from the Crimea, defeated soldiers turned down-at-heel, starving wretches. But this happened somewhat later. I spent the spring and summer of 1920 wandering around Sebastopol, patronizing cafés and theatres, and amazing "Oriental cellars" where people consumed *chebureki* and soured milk, where with Olympian serenity swarthy Armenians gazed upon officers' drunken tears as they gulped down desperate alcoholic concoctions and crooned unsteadily "God Save the Tsar", which sounded at once plaintive and indecent, having lost its meaning long ago and died in that Oriental cellar, where, from the barracks of Petersburg, the musical grandeur of a fallen empire now abased itself: it slid along smoke-begrimed walls and got stuck between the Georgian breasts of painted nudes, beauties with broad rumps and equine eyes, who emitted remarkably smooth, woody streams of tobacco smoke from their hookahs. All the woe of provincial Russia, all its eternal melancholy filled Sebastopol. In the theatres, Odessan artistes with aristocratic pseudonyms sang chesty romances, which, completely independent of their content, always sounded extraordinarily wistful; and they met with great success. I saw tears in the eyes of usually unsentimental people; revolution, having deprived them of their homes, families and repasts, suddenly offered them the capacity to feel profound grief and for an instant liberated from their coarse, bellicose exterior their long-forgotten, long-lost spiritual sensitivity. It was as if these people were taking part in a concert performance of a silent symphony written in a minor key; for the first time they saw that they had a biography, a history of their lives, and a lost happiness which until then they had only read about in books. And the Black Sea seemed to me like an enormous Babylonian river basin, and the clay mountains of Sebastopol the ancient wailing wall. Hot waves of air rolled over the town—and suddenly the wind got up, raising ripples on the water and reminding me of my inevitable departure. People had already begun talking about exit passports and packing up their belongings; but after a short while the armoured train was sent back to the front; and so we left, gazing back at the sea, plunging into black tunnels and returning once more to those hostile Russian expanses that we had escaped with such difficulty the previous winter. It was the White Army's final offensive: it was short-lived, and before long the troops were once again fleeing south along frozen highways. During those months the army's fate concerned me less than it had done before. I didn't think about it. On the platform of the armoured train I journeyed past scorched fields and golden trees, past coppices by the side of the rails; and in the autumn I was sent on a mission to Sebastopol, which I found slightly changed, for it was already the beginning of October. There I very nearly drowned, crossing the bay in a shoddy motorboat from the north side to the south—during a storm; and, after being in Sebastopol for several days, I headed back to the armoured train, which in my imagination was just as I had left it, while in actual fact it had been captured by the Red Army along with the base; the crew had deserted—and only thirty-odd soldiers and officers had somehow managed to retreat along with the remaining forces: they placed themselves into one of the heated freight cars and lurched around there, blankly gazing upon the red walls and not quite understanding that there was no longer any armoured train, any army, that Chub, our best gunner, had been killed, that Filippenko was dead, his leg having been blown off, that the sailor Vanya, who was a most articulate blasphemer, was now in captivity, and that the entire supply section, from the porter Mikhutin down to a turkey, a live pig, several calves and horses—all in that marvellous zoological state to which they were accustomed—also no longer existed. Lapshin, a friend of mine, who even in the heated freight car would not be parted from his mandolin, playing now "The Funeral March", now "The Little Apple", would blithely say:

"If the turkey and the pig have died, unable to endure this turn of the wheel of history, then what hope do we have?… All we can do is to keep going…"

Many had stayed behind, not wanting to retreat—some even headed north, to the Red Army. On board one of the oncoming trains they spotted Vorobyov in a railwayman's service cap with its red peak; vanishing slowly into the distance, he was shaking his fist and crying in a long, drawn-out manner: swine! swine!—as though he were on a raft, floating down a river or across a lake, and had to strain his voice.

The train I had taken to meet the retreating forces stopped at a little halt and would go no farther. Nobody knew why the train was at a standstill. Then I heard a conversation between an officer and the train's superintendent. The officer was saying hurriedly:

"No, you tell me why we aren't moving. No, I'm asking you, why in the devil's name are we stuck here? No, I won't stand for this, you know. No, you answer me…"

"We can't go any further: the Reds are behind us," another voice answered.

"Behind us isn't in front. If they were in front, we really wouldn't be able to move forward. But, you see, damn it, we're not moving backwards, are we?"

"I can't let the train go."

"Why in blazes not?"

"There are Reds behind us."

Violent cursing ensued, after which the superintendent said in an imploring voice: "I can't go, there are Reds behind us." He kept repeating this phrase, because he was in the grip of deathly terror; he believed that wherever he went the same fate was awaiting him: he had ceased to understand, but was refusing to move, irrationally, like an animal being pulled on a leash. And so the train went nowhere. I transferred to one of the carriages in the light armoured train *Yaroslav the Wise*, which was standing alongside ours. And since I hadn't slept for two nights, I fell asleep the moment I lay down on a bunk. I dreamt of Elizaveta Mikhaylovna, who metamorphosed into a

Spaniard with clacking castanets. She danced, completely naked, to the music of an extraordinarily loud orchestra; and amid the terrible din, loudest of all came the deep growling of a double bass and the piercing high notes of a French horn. The noise became unbearable; and when I opened my eyes, I heard the growling of a tame bear, which, dragging its long chain across the floor, was thrashing back and forth about the carriage. Sometimes it would stop and start swaying from side to side. There was no one in the carriage but me, the bear and some peasant woman in a shawl; Lord knows how and why she had wound up there—she was awfully frightened and was wailing loudly and crying. It had just begun to grow light. The windows rang and shattered, a wind blew: the armoured train was under intensive machine-gun fire. "Budyonny's men!" the peasant woman cried. "Budyonny's men!" Not far from us the six-inch guns of a naval battery thundered their heavy response to the Red artillery bombardment. I went out onto the platform and saw, half a verst from the base, the grey mass of Budyonny's cavalry. The bombardment filled the air with groaning and rumbling. Nearby I heard the sound of an incoming medium-calibre shell—and judging by the noise, it was easy to determine that the shell would land on either our carriage or the neighbouring one; and so, as the woman fell silent, unconsciously submitting to the sense of spiritual and physical calm that precedes the moment of some terrible event, I realized that she—though knowing nothing of those differing tones in the shrieking of projectiles by which artillerymen can tell approximately where the explosion will come—sensed the terrific danger threatening her. But the shell hit the neighbouring carriage, which was full of wounded officers; a whole wave of cries immediately issued from there—as happens at a concert when the conductor, with a deft movement, suddenly jabs his baton into the left or right wing of the orchestra, from where an entire fountain of sound instantly gushes up with the swell and fluttering of strings. The six-inch guns launched a never-ending volley of shells directly upon the black mass of men and horses—and pieces of black debris flashed in the pillars of smoke raised by the explosions.

I stood there on the platform, looking ahead and freezing in the sixteen degrees of frost—and I dreamt of my snug berth in the base of the armoured train, the electric lamp, my books, a hot shower and a warm bed. I knew that the part of the train where I found myself was surrounded, cut off by Budyonny's cavalry, that they had enough shells for another few hours and that sooner or later, though no later than that evening, we would be killed or captured. I knew this perfectly well, but the dream of warmth and books and white bed linen so preoccupied me that I had no time to think of anything else; rather, this dream was the most delightful and beautiful of all my remaining thoughts, and I could not bear to part with it. The black rain of explosions and various sounds—from the dry scraping of bullets against stone and the resilient ringing of the rails and carriage wheels to the deep reverberations of cannon fire and human cries—all this converged without blending into one noise, each series of sounds retaining its own independent existence. All this went on from early morning until three or four o'clock in the afternoon. I would return to the carriage only to leave it again, unable to get warm or to fall asleep—until at last I saw black specks on the horizon approaching the battlefield. "Red cavalry!" someone shouted. "It's over!" But just as relentlessly the cannon and machine guns fired, subsiding every now and then like a mighty downpour that would resume with the first gust of wind. An old officer, an intendant colonel with a tearful face, passed me by several times, evidently not knowing where he was going or why. One soldier crawled under the carriage and rolled a cigarette with fingers that were blue from the cold, immediately exhaling a whole cloud of acrid tobacco smoke. "The bullets won't get me down here, old chap," he told me with a grin when I bent down to take a look at him. All of a sudden, however, the fighting began to abate; the shots grew less frequent. Cavalry was bearing down upon us from the north. Having climbed up onto the roof of the train, I saw clearly the horses and their riders, a dense wall of which was galloping towards us. Hiding between the buffers, the old colonel was crying: beside him, clutching the end of his yellow bashlyk, stood a little girl of about eight, all bundled up; the soldier's cigarette smoke, which seemed to be coming from below ground, was quickly borne away by the wind. Before long, I could hear the clatter of hooves, and after several minutes of agonized waiting, as at the theatre, hundreds of riders made their final approach. The mass of Budyonny's cavalry began to quicken their pace; we heard cries, and soon everything was set in motion: Budyonny's troops began to retreat, and the cavalry that had arrived from the north followed after them. Not far from me an officer in a Circassian coat galloped by, turning around every second and shouting something; and I saw that not only did the soldiers following him not understand a thing, but also he himself did not know what it was that he was trying to say or why. Immediately after that, I again caught sight of the old colonel who had just been crying; now wearing a look of importance and intent, he was making his way towards his heated freight car. Meanwhile, the smoke from under the carriage had stopped; the soldier emerged and called out to me: "Well, thank God for that!"—before running off somewhere.

After a day of wandering among the countless carriages, goods trains and carts, I found the forty men who continued to call themselves the armoured train *Smoke*, although that train itself no longer existed. With each coming hour the army dwindled; its carts rattled along the frosty road, the army vanished into the horizon, and its noise and movement were carried off with the strong wind. This was on the 16th and 17th of October, and in the last week of that same month, when I found myself sitting in a village hut not far from Theodosia, eating bread and jam, washing it down with warm milk in a room filled with excited and smiling faces, in walked my comrade-in-arms Mitya the Marquess. He was given this moniker because, when the boys had asked him one day which book he liked best, he named a novel by an unknown but undoubtedly fine French writer—and that novel was called *The Destitute Countess*. I read it once, because Mitya had brought it with him. The main characters were persons of title, and Mitya was incapable of reading such books without great emotion, though he himself was a native of Ekaterinoslav Governorate, had never seen a big city, and hadn't the slightest idea what France was like. Yet for him the words "marquess", "count" and especially "baronet" were filled with a deep meaning—hence he was dubbed "the Marquess". "They've taken Dzhankoy," said Mitya the Marquess with innate delight—something he experienced even when announcing the most tragic news. Indeed, any major event stirred in him the happy feeling that he, Mitya the Marquess, had again escaped unscathed; and since such great events had indeed begun to happen, it followed that even more excitement lay ahead. I remember that in the most testing of circumstances, even when somebody had been killed or mortally wounded, Mitya the Marquess would say with excitement, panting in order to hide his laughter: "Filippenko's had his leg torn off. Chernousov's been wounded in the stomach, and Lieutenant Sanin in his left arm: there's fate for you!"

"They've taken Dzhankoy; things must be going badly," said Mitya.

Indeed, Dzhankoy had once stood on our side of the fortifications in the Crimea. Dzhankoy: the kerosene lamps on the station platform, the women who would come to our carriage, the beefsteaks from the station's snack bar, Caesar's commentaries, Lavinov, my dreams—and Elizaveta Mikhaylovna in my dreams. Past the village, one after another, four trains sped in the direction of Theodosia. After a journey of several hours, we too found ourselves there. It was evening, and we were billeted in an empty shop whose bare shelves served as our beds. The windows of the shop had been smashed; the hollow echo of our conversations resounded in the empty storerooms, and it seemed that it was other people talking and arguing alongside us, our doubles—and their words carried an indisputable melancholy gravitas that we ourselves lacked; but the echo elevated our voices, made our phrases more drawn-out, and as we listened to it, it slowly dawned on us that something irrevocable had happened. With clarity we heard what we should never have known had it not been for that echo. We saw that we would leave; but we understood this only as an immediate prospect, and our imaginations stretched no further than the sea and the ship, while the echo carried something new and unfamiliar, as though reaching us from those countries we had not yet visited but were now destined to know.

As I stood on the deck of the ship and looked out over a burning Theodosia—there was a fire in the town—I didn't think that I was leaving my country, nor did I feel it until I remembered Claire. "Claire," I said to myself, and instantly I saw her in the fur cloud of her winter coat. Fire and water separated me from my country and Claire's—and so Claire vanished behind fiery walls.

For a long while afterwards, the shores of Russia haunted the ship: phosphorite sand rained down on the sea, dolphins leapt in the water, the propellers turned silently and the sides of the ship creaked; and down below, in the brig, there was the sobbing babble of women and the sound of the grain with which the ship was laden. The fire in Theodosia looked more distant and weaker now; the noise of the engine grew louder and more distinct; and then, coming to for the first time, I marked that Russia was gone and that we were sailing upon a sea, surrounded by nocturnal blue water, beneath whose surface the backs of dolphins could be glimpsed—and under a sky that was closer to us than ever before.

"But Claire is French," I suddenly recalled, "and if this is so, then what was all that constant, intense sorrow about snow and green plains for, all that sorrow for those many lives I had lived in a country now hidden from me behind a fiery curtain?" I began to dream of meeting Claire in Paris, where she had been born, and where she would undoubtedly return. Before my eyes I saw France, Claire's native land, and Paris, and the place de la Concorde; and the square seemed different to me from the one I had seen depicted on postcards—the one with lamps and fountains and naïve figures, the water constantly running and streaming down those figures, glistening darkly. Yes, the place de la Concorde suddenly seemed different to me. It had always existed inside me; I had often imagined Claire and myself there—but the echoes and images of my former life didn't penetrate there, as though they had come up against an invisible wall of air—of air, but just as insuperable as that barricade of fire behind which snow covered the earth and the last nocturnal alarms of Russia sounded. They rang the bells on the ship, and the tolling instantly reminded me of the bay in Sebastopol as it lay covered in a great multitude of ships illumined by little lights, and on each of these ships the bells would ring the hour—hollow and cracked on some, faint on others, resounding on others still. The tolling rang out over the sea, over the waves slick with oil. The water lapped at the quay, and by night the port of Sebastopol recalled those paintings of far-flung Japanese harbours asleep above a yellow ocean—so subtle, so inscrutable to my reason. I saw Japanese harbours and slender girls in paper houses, their delicate fingers and narrow eyes, and it seemed to me that I had divined in them that particular combination of chastity and shamelessness that forced travellers and adventurers to set their sights upon these yellow shores, upon this Mongolian sorcery, as fragile and sonorous as air that has turned into stained glass. For a long time we sailed across the Black Sea; it was cold, and

I sat wrapped in my greatcoat, dreaming of Japanese harbours, of beaches in Borneo and Sumatra, while the landscape of a flat sandy shore along which lofty palm trees grew never left my mind. Much later I had occasion to hear the music of these islands, a drawn-out, vibrating sound, like that of a shaking saw, which I still remembered from the time when I was all of three years old. Then, in a flood of sudden happiness, I felt an infinitely complex and ambrosial feeling that reflected the Indian Ocean, the palms, the olive-skinned women, the blazing tropical sun and the humid undergrowth of southern plants concealing serpents' heads with little eyes; a yellow mist rose up over this tropical verdure, curling magically before dispersing—and once again that drawn-out sound of a shaking saw, having crossed thousands upon thousands of versts, transported me to the frozen waters of Petersburg, which the divine power of sound again transformed into a distant landscape of islands in the Indian Ocean; and just as in childhood, in Father's tales, the Indian Ocean opened up a life unknown to me, rising up over the hot sand and soaring like the wind over the palms.

To the tolling of the ship's bell we sailed for Constantinople, and even then, on board the ship, I had begun to lead a new existence, one in which all my attention and cares were turned to my future meeting with

Claire, in France, whither I would go from old Stamboul. My mind begot thousands of imagined situations and conversations, each one interrupted and superseded by others, though the loveliest thought was that Claire, whom I had left behind that winter's night, Claire, whose shadow eclipses me and whose memory causes everything around me to sound quieter and muted—that this Claire would be mine. And once again her unattainable body, still more impossible than ever, appeared before me at the stern of the ship littered with sleeping bodies, guns and knapsacks. But then the sky clouded over, the stars disappeared from view, and we found ourselves sailing in the marine twilight towards an invisible city; airy precipices yawned behind us, and from time to time the tolling of a bell could be heard amid the humid still of the journey—and this sound which faithfully accompanied us, the lone sound of a bell, united in its slow glass-like transparency the fiery brinks and the water separating me from Russia with a murmuring, straying, beautiful dream of Claire.

PARIS, JULY 1929

NOTES

1 *Heureux acquéreurs… constructeur*: Happy buyers of a genuine Salamander / never abandoned by the maker.

2 *mais vous êtes fou*: You're mad.

3 *mon Dieu, qu'il est simple!*: Heavens, how naïve he is!

4 *Oui, mon petit… là*: Yes, my dear, it's very interesting what you're saying there.

5 *Asseyez-vous ici*: Sit here.

6 *Oui, mon petit… quand même*: Yes, my dear, it's sad. What an unhappy pair we make.

7 *J'étais… d'habitude*: You surprised me just then. I thought you always kept your cigarettes on you, in your trouser pocket. Have you changed your habit?

8 *Dites-moi… un pantalon*: Tell me, what is the difference between a trench coat and a pair of trousers?

9 *Je ne vous reconnais pas… distraire*: I scarcely recognize you, my dear. Anyway, why don't you set the gramophone going? That will distract you.

10 *C'est une chemise rose… champs*: It's a pink shirt / with a little lady inside, / fresh as a blossoming bud, / simple as a wildflower.

11 *Il n'y manque qu'une chose*: There's only one thing missing.

12 *Non, ce n'est pas bien dit, ça*: No, that isn't witty.

13 *Mais qu'est-ce que vous avez… comme toujours*: Whatever is the matter with you tonight? You aren't quite yourself.

14 *Mais entrez donc… thé*: Come in. You'll have a cup of tea.

15 *Comment ne compreniez vous pas*: How could you not understand?…

16 *Vous ne dormez pas... le matin*: Can't you sleep? Sleep, my darling, you'll be tired in the morning.

17 *Je ne sais... se tenir*: I cannot fathom why you're forever inviting young men, like this one here, with his soiled, unbuttoned shirt, who doesn't even know how to conduct himself.

18 *Ce jeune home... le français*: This young man understands French perfectly well.

19 *Oh, laissez-moi tranquille tous*: Oh, just leave me alone, all of you!

20 *Claire n'est plus vierge*: Claire is a virgin no more.

PUSHKIN PRESS

Pushkin Press was founded in 1997, and publishes novels, essays, memoirs, children's books—everything from timeless classics to the urgent and contemporary.

This book is part of the Pushkin Collection of paperbacks, designed to be as satisfying as possible to hold and to enjoy. It is typeset in Monotype Baskerville, based on the transitional English serif typeface designed in the mid-eighteenth century by John Baskerville. It was litho-printed on Munken Premium White Paper and notch-bound by the independently owned printer TJ International in Padstow, Cornwall. The cover, with French flaps, was printed on Rives Linear Bright White paper. The paper and cover board are both acid-free and Forest Stewardship Council (FSC) certified.

Pushkin Press publishes the best writing from around the world—great stories, beautifully produced, to be read and read again.

STEFAN ZWEIG · EDGAR ALLAN POE · ISAAC BABEL
TOMÁS GONZÁLEZ · ULRICH PLENZDORF · JOSEPH KESSEL
VELIBOR ČOLIĆ · LOUISE DE VILMORIN · MARCEL AYMÉ
ALEXANDER PUSHKIN · MAXIM BILLER · JULIEN GRACQ
BROTHERS GRIMM · HUGO VON HOFMANNSTHAL
GEORGE SAND · PHILIPPE BEAUSSANT · IVÁN REPILA
E.T.A. HOFFMANN · ALEXANDER LERNET-HOLENIA
YASUSHI INOUE · HENRY JAMES · FRIEDRICH TORBERG
ARTHUR SCHNITZLER · ANTOINE DE SAINT-EXUPÉRY
MACHI TAWARA · GAITO GAZDANOV · HERMANN HESSE
LOUIS COUPERUS · JAN JACOB SLAUERHOFF
PAUL MORAND · MARK TWAIN · PAUL FOURNEL
ANTAL SZERB · JONA OBERSKI · MEDARDO FRAILE
HÉCTOR ABAD · PETER HANDKE · ERNST WEISS
PENELOPE DELTA · RAYMOND RADIGUET · PETR KRÁL
ITALO SVEVO · RÉGIS DEBRAY · BRUNO SCHULZ · TEFFI
EGON HOSTOVSKÝ · JOHANNES URZIDIL · JÓZEF WITTLIN